To the Whiskey Crew 12

Your wisdom, sacrifice and devotion to this country inspires me to be better every day. Your integrity and character is the blood that runs through Chad's veins and the breath in his lungs.

To J.C., K.D., F.K, T.D. and B.O, the surviving members of WC12, this series is to honor your continued sacrifice and honor the lives we lost. I am forever grateful to call you friends and guardians.

chapter *one*

HOPE

*C*OFFEE. COFFEE WAS LIFE. COFFEE was the blood that ran through her veins. Really, it ran through the veins of those that came through the doors of Koffeehaus, Hope figured. She was struggling to lock the finicky door at 8:30 PM; well really, it was 8:25 PM, but she never had any customers pounding at the door during close. Until today. Hope squinted her eyes, seeing the headlights of a large, silver truck pull in. She instantly smiled, waving, even though she couldn't see the driver.

Hope was mildly disappointed earlier when her favorite customer, Chad Turner, hadn't shown up for his usual cup of coffee and chat on Monday afternoon. This disappointment faded as she unlocked the door and turned to head toward the coffee counter to provide Chad some privacy since he typically changed out of his uniform in the truck. He was a United States Marine and regulation called for them to not wear their utilities, or their camouflage uniform, off-base.

Once behind the counter, she turned the switch on for the water to begin to boil for a fresh cup of coffee for him, and then turned her attention to herself, absentmindedly dusting off the black apron that clung to her small frame. By the end of the day, all sources of flour and sugar always found their way to the front of her apron.

She chided herself for going the extra mile to make sure she looked presentable, reminding herself that he was no more than another customer. Just another customer that reminded her that butterflies still existed. As she tucked blonds wisps of hair behind her ear, the overhead bell rang, signaling Chad's entrance. She leaned over the counter to greet him. There he was, in all his fine form, those broad shoulders, hugged by a dark green cotton t-shirt. He always wore rugged dark jeans with a belt, too. She still couldn't figure out how he changed so quickly in his truck. He was handsome, with light brown hair cut short, very fit, and just tall enough that Hope would have to stand on her tippy toes to reach him. *Not that she thought about that often.* She couldn't help but grin at her inner thought.

It wasn't his body that made her heart skip, but his dazzling smile. His smile reached his eyes, and it always sent a brilliant feeling down her spine when he greeted her.

"Hey Chad, I was closing up early. I'm glad you pulled up when you did."

"Hey there, Hope. Me too." Chad strode into the quaint coffeehouse, passing the lounge area, and another area with wooden chairs and tables displayed haphazardly. "You still have any coffee left? I'll take anything, I've got duty tonight and need liquid gold, STAT." He leaned over the counter and sighed, running his hand across his face. It was clear he was tired. She could tell by the small lines of fatigue he had in his forehead on days like these.

"I just started the water. Coffee coming right up." Hope cocked her head as she reached over and patted his hand that rested on the counter. "Bad day?" *Wait, was it okay to touch him?* she chided herself again. *Don't touch the customers...but he isn't like the other customers. Stop. Stop, Hope.* She continued mentally scolding herself, when the sound of the water coming to a boil pulled her out of her rebuking moment. Chad smiled back at her as she let go of his hand, and turned to pour hot water over the fresh grinds. If he noticed her blush, he didn't call her on it.

He always chose the Americano, and she always made sure it was in stock, and fresh. She tried convincing herself that it was for all the customers but, in reality, it was for him. Hope filled the mug as she listened to Chad give her the rundown of his day. She always attempted to follow Chad's descriptions of his daily duties and for the most part, she thought she understood, but there were times where she just tried to put the pieces together to make a half-assed response.

"Well, Chad. Is there any way you can get someone else to do all the reports, so you can get ahead on the logistical stuff?" she asked, in an attempt to help, as she watched him take the full mug of coffee to the condiment bar. She couldn't help but smile as he poured sugar into his coffee; they often joked he preferred coffee-flavored sugar more than coffee.

"Not exactly. I wish that was how it worked. At least I have duty tonight. I'll get ahead that way." Chad sounded resigned when he returned to the counter, but his dazzling smile held steady. He spent much of his time off-base time in Koffeehaus with Hope. At least, that's what Hope imagined.

Hope had many Marine customers. She gladly served the men and women, and enthusiastically befriended many too, but Chad was different. Whenever he came in for his coffee, he lingered, talking as time allowed. She had enjoyed their conversations, from the first day they met. She turned away from the front of the counter to pour herself a decaffeinated cup of coffee from the batch she made earlier.

"Are you copping out?" Chad jested. "Decaf? It's only 8:30."

She rolled her eyes at him playfully. "If I had caffeine right now, I would be up for hours. I have nothing better to do than sleep tonight, unlike you." She grinned at him, but there was a small pang that lingered from her past. She used to have coffee on her writing sprint nights. It would guarantee her long hours of writing, a bliss she refused to experience again.

She did a very good job hiding her pain. It had been several months since she moved to Jacksonville, North Carolina, but the grief rose its ugly head at the weirdest moments. She did her best not to let it rise right now.

Chad shook his head at her response. "Yes, that's for sure. I have duty until oh four hundred. I had the shitty block." He took a long swig from the cup, while she admired the way his muscles tensed when he did. She had goosebumps simply from watching him. "Hey, at least you aren't tainting your coffee with cream."

She shifted her weight back over the counter to be across from him, letting out a soft laugh at his reference and mockingly responded, "The only place you find cream in coffee is in hell." This provoked a deep laugh from Chad, one she enjoyed.

"Good girl, you remembered." He winked at her. *Oh, those winks.* Those winks made her weak.

The only thing she could do was hold the mug with both hands, close to herself, as they each leaned over the counter, letting silence sink in. They were okay with pauses; it was natural for them. Making eye contact with him, she asked, "I'm not rushing you out, I promise. Stay as long as you like, but do you mind if I start cleaning up?"

Chad waved her on teasingly. "I see how it is. You get called out for your weak coffee moves and you take it out on me." He paused for a moment, before continuing, "Of course. Don't let me get in the way."

She shook her head. "Not at all. I typically put some music on, though. Do you have a preference?" Although they had been talking for a few months, there were still plenty of things they didn't know about each other. But, little by little, they conquered one topic at a time. Today, it was music.

"I will never turn down music. Feeds the soul. Whatever your favorite playlist is. I'm interested." He grinned at her, taking his mug from the counter and moving to one of the arm chairs. She had already made her way to the back to grab her phone to connect to the Koffeehaus speakers. Mrs. Lulu, the older woman who owned the coffeehouse, preferred no music, but allowed her and Em, her coworker who opened the coffeehouse each day, to play whatever music they wanted, so long as the customers didn't complain. Mrs. Lulu, a wonderful woman, and hero to Hope, was flexible with how the shop was run. The customers came first, and so did the coffee. Hope loved the concept.

Chewing on her bottom lip, she contemplated which playlist she should stream. She settled on her mixed playlist of some oldies but goodies and modern top hits. *I hope he isn't disappointed.* She loved all kinds of music, from classic rock to current top 100 hits. Hopefully Chad wouldn't mind.

Once music began playing, she peeked over the counter to gauge Chad's response to the first song, "Stairway to Heaven." It was also one her mother loved. That pang rose again, but she swallowed it down when she saw Chad give her a thumbs-up. "Not bad taste. You can never go wrong with Led Zeppelin."

Hope smiled as she picked up the rag to start cleaning. "Good, but fair warning. Britney Spears and Lady Gaga will have their time too." She laughed as she leaned over the different equipment and surfaces to sanitize and clean.

Chad struck his palm to his forehead. "And here I was, giving you credit for your taste. All that negates this song all together, woman," he teased as she watched him take the last sip of his coffee.

She waved her hand over the counter to him. "Give me your mug, I'll give you a refill in a to-go cup."

He hoisted himself out of the arm chair and moved to the counter, planting the empty mug in her hand. "Do I need to go?" Chad questioned curiously. "I don't want you breaking any rules on my part; I was the one who showed up late."

Hope shook her head quickly at him, waving a hand as she started the hot water again. "No, no. You said you had duty. I figured I would keep you filled until you had to go. It takes me about an hour or so to clean up and close, so hang out as long as you like." She smiled at him as she poured the hot water over the fresh grinds. Mrs. Lulu used the pour over method, a simple yet classic way to capture coffee flavor. "It also lets me wash your mug and have it done before we open tomorrow. I try not to leave anything overnight." Hope slid the cup over to him.

"Ditto. I can appreciate the efficiency." He took the cup and offered her a grateful nod as he deeply inhaled the strong aroma. "This shit is just too good not to have around. I need to stock up before field training and deployment. Remind me?" He grinned at her as he made his way back to the condiment bar.

Hope laughed, shaking her head. "I'll set some aside for you. When do you leave?" she asked as she cleaned the equipment, leaving the grinder, and water machine for his last refill. They were easiest to clean last.

He returned to the counter, while she paused to admire the way he delicately stirred his coffee with a wooden stirrer. It was as if he had a certain number of rotations before he knew the sugar and coffee was set right. "I have field training every four to six weeks, I go out next in two weeks." He looked into his cup and then took his first sip. With a grin, she made her way around the counter to retrieve the cream and milk pitchers from the condiment bar. She would make sure to have some packaged.

"So, Hope. My question of the day for you. Are you ready?" He leaned his hip against the counter, facing her as she cleaned the condiment bar and picked up the pitchers.

"Ready as I'll ever be." She loved his daily questions. It was his way of getting to know her, at least that is what she thought. *Hopefully.*

"Answer honestly. Who is your favorite customer, and why?" He paused for a moment. "Outside of me, of course." He teased her with a wink and one of his signature grins. She was going to faint.

You. You are my favorite customer. But I can't say that. Her thoughts overruled and she selected her favorite couple. "Mr. and Mrs. Paisley." She paused, only for a moment, before she began cleaning again. "They're an older couple, maybe in their eighties, and that's me being generous.

They come in during the afternoon lull to share a bakery item and have tea with each other." She smiled reminiscently as she talked about the Paisleys who visited Koffeehaus. "They've been married sixty years and have five children. Mr. Paisley was fifteen when he forged his way into the military to fight in World War II." Hope carried the pitchers of dairy behind the counter to clean. She couldn't help but think they would be amazing characters for a book... but stopped her thought process. There was no writing for her. She left that part of her behind when she moved.

"I know the Paisleys. Everyone knows them. They owned several of the restaurants and stores here. They have quite the legacy here in Jax." He sipped his coffee, and she hoped he didn't have the ability to read her mind.

She smiled as she turned the water on, the loud sound from the pressure drowning their conversation, and Hope's thoughts of pursuing writing again as well. She watched the water and her dream swirl down the drain. She was always amazed at how a split second, a moment in time, could change the trajectory of one's life in such a fast way. She shook her head, unnoticeably to Chad, and hung the pitchers up on the hooks to dry, ready for Em in the morning.

She turned around to be greeted by one of his smaller, but sweet smiles. "I better go." He checked his watch, as if he didn't know what time it was. "Duty calls. Literally." He lifted his mug up in a feigned toast. "How much do I owe you?" He sat it down and reached in his back pocket for his wallet.

"It is on the house. I've zeroed the register already," she fibbed.

"For some reason, I doubt that, but thank you for the

generous refill too." He smiled as he tucked his wallet back in his pocket. "Will you be safe this late?" He looked out the window at the darkness outside.

"Oh yes, no one will bother me here." She came around the counter to join him, walking to the door. "I have never felt afraid." That was the truth.

"Good." He smiled as they reached the door. He pulled the door open, and turned to pause in what Hope thought was a reluctance to leave, then he waved. "Have a good night, Hope."

"Good night, Chad. I hope duty is uneventful." Chad turned and grinned at her one more time, as she waved back. She stayed at the door until she saw him pull away from the small building, offering one last wave before returning to her cleaning duties. Damn. He always made her feel so good.

chapter two

CHAD

*T*WO WEEKS LATER, CHAD CRANED backwards, stretching his arm to the back seat of his truck. He was glad he had the extended cab, for all the crap he hauled around - such as an extra change of clothing. He pulled up a green shirt, inspected it before he pressed it to his nose to smell. It was clean. Good! He pulled his uniform top off, straining on each side to remove the jacket from his body. He unceremoniously grabbed the back neck of his green colored t-shirt and pulled it over his head. He quickly replaced it with a light green cotton t-shirt, smoothing the sleeves and back as much as he could in a seated position in a pickup truck.

Now the jeans were a different story. He had mastered the lower body dressing while seated in Officer Commissioning School, or OCS. He didn't like to ever talk about how or why he had to learn this technique, but he was quick to change his pants. He pushed his door open after successfully buttoning his fly. He kicked his boots off and laid back to reach for his sneakers he tucked on the floor of the passenger side backseat. Tying the laces, he placed the boots back into the truck and jumped down. Grabbing his wallet from the dashboard, he shut and locked the truck door and made his way toward the coffeehouse.

He peeked through the brightly-lit windows to see Hope wiping down the condiment counter. He smiled, watching her work so skillfully - her blonde hair shifting over her shoulder as she managed to clean the counter. He always liked the way she tucked the stray hairs behind her ear when they talked.

He blinked and looked around, realizing he would look like a creep peering in a window if he didn't enter the coffeehouse soon. He pushed through the glass door, listening for that familiar bell tone. He smiled seeing her finishing the cleaning task and turn to face him.

"Hey Chad!" She offered him a bright smile. *She's happy to see me.* Chad made his way to the counter to put in his daily order. He admired the way Hope moved. It was as if she was floating. It was either that or he was just watching her too closely.

"Hey Hope. How was your day?" He leaned over the counter and smiled at her. Her face was a light flushed color. She must've been doing more than wiping counters before he walked in.

She smiled at him as she tapped his usual order, without asking, into the flat screen tablet, flipping it over for him to complete the order. "Busy. Very busy today. I saw a lot of new faces. There's either a new group here for training or you guys are rotating." He watched her turn to fix his drink before he even finished sliding his card.

He laughed. "You've already picked up on the changing faces. There are always new faces coming and going; never a lull." He couldn't help but admire her from behind. He was a man, after all. Or at least, that's the excuse he wanted to use today. He shook his head before she turned around so he could focus on the conversation.

"And you? How was your day?" Hope turned around and slid the mug across the counter to him, their fingers grazing for a moment. The skin underneath her touch tingled. "I'm going to make a cup for myself," she commented as she turned back around, and he moved the mug over to the condiment counter to use the sugar. They were both diverting attention from the momentary touch.

"Same shit, different day." He poured the sugar in as he glanced back over at her. He returned the sugar back to standing position, before he over poured it by being distracted, watching Hope. He couldn't help but watch her sip her coffee. She held the mug by the handle and used the other hand to hug it. It was endearing. Apparently, his brain wanted to make something as simple as drinking coffee, into something dirty and lustful.

"Aren't you going out soon?" Hope asked, interrupting his mental interlude.

He returned to the counter to face her, his hand covering his mug as if he was preserving the heat while he answered, "Yes, you have a really sharp memory. Training this weekend for a few weeks." He nodded, and then shook his head at the prospect of being trapped on base for three weeks, without an opportunity to visit her. "It shouldn't be too bad. The Majors have most of their shit together this time around."

"Well, that's good." She had an uncanny way of watching him enjoy his coffee that made his body very aware of her presence. He wished he could read her mind. He almost choked from laughing, when she popped up from her position, recalling something she'd apparently wanted to tell him, as she set her coffee mug down. "I almost forgot! I talked to Mrs. Lulu about you wanting coffee while you're out, since you love it so much. She made you something, and you should take it today before I forget for real!" He watched her petite form quickly glide across the floor behind the counter to disappear into the stockroom.

He continued to drink his coffee, listening to her rummage in the room, returning with a box almost as big as she was. "Woah there! Let me get that." He set his mug down to take the box from her. "What is this?" Curiosity caught ahold of him.

"Open it! It's her – well, she says our, but really from her - gift to you and your unit for training, or deployment, or whenever you want it." She clasped her hands together excitedly, much like a child on Christmas day. He smiled at her amusement and anticipation. *She must like surprises.*

He slid his finger underneath the loose tape holding the top open and peeked into the box. The aroma of coffee struck him before he could make out what was in it. They had donated at least thirty pounds of freshly ground coffee, Americano nonetheless. His smile grew from their generosity. "Wow! You are fucking amazing. The guys, wait, no, *I* will forever be grateful for this. Thank you!" He slid the top closed to re-tape it gingerly. He looked over at her behind the counter, and winked. "Can I get a hug for this?"

He watched her absorb the request for a split second before quickly sliding her mug back on the counter. "Oh, absolutely. But really, it wasn't me, it was Mrs. Lulu." As she approached him, she opened her arms to reach for him. He wrapped his arms around her small waist and pulled her into a warm hug. Her full body against his, made his skin prickle with desire.

chapter *three*

HOPE

*T*HE LIGHT TRICKLED IN THROUGH the sheer curtains, splaying across her cheeks. Hope's eyes fluttered at Mother Nature's wake-up call. She rolled over from her side to her back, stretching her arms over her head and taking in the morning moment. Mmm. Saturday. The sweet sound of silence was brilliant. She pushed herself up into a sitting position, tilting her head against the wall serving as her bed's headboard. Hope looked out the window through the long white sheer fabric, assessing the sunlight and estimating the weather. She smiled when she saw the butterflies gathering around the wildflowers that grew along the border of the property. She was certain the peonies that lined the side of the house, Mrs. Lulu's favorite flowers, were covered in ladybugs. This was a wonderful spring; the news reported a huge influx of butterflies and ladybugs, for absolutely no natural reason. She would enjoy them while they were here.

It was a beautiful day and she was determined to enjoy it. She planned on catching up on some housework she'd been neglecting, and she carved out some time in her day to sit on the porch and play her guitar. On her way home from Koffeehaus last night, she stopped at the music shop near the small house she rented and picked up her guitar. She had dropped it off to have it repaired and restrung; it was banged up from her drive to Jacksonville. Hope regretted the neglect the guitar suffered, but she made up for it in the brand-new finish and strings she purchased. She may have given up writing, but her soul was content with her guitar.

Hope lazily slid out from underneath the dark blue covers and sauntered into her tiny bathroom. Leaning over the sink, she looked at herself in the mirror. She pulled her hair up into a messy bun and started to wash her face. She was finally beginning to pick herself up from the pit that she landed in months ago.

A fresh start was what she was looking for in Jacksonville, and she'd found it with a little help from Mrs. Lulu. Not only was Mrs. Lulu her employer, but the tiny house she was living in belonged to the gracious woman as well. It had two bedrooms, a small living space, kitchen, and tiny fenced-in backyard, with a porch to match. She enjoyed the quaintness of Mrs. Lulu's home and was thankful Mrs. Lulu had been willing to rent it to her for very little.

She was adding her own touches slowly, like her favorite paintings she brought from home, as well as some random splashes of blue and gold throughout the house. She didn't know why Mrs. Lulu had so much faith in her, even when she had been transparent with her own shortcomings, but her new boss and landlord stepped in with a warm, maternal input. Mrs. Lulu frequently visited during the day to keep her company when the coffee shop was slow, and their friendship continued to grow with time. Mrs. Lulu took a chance on her and she would forever be grateful for the generosity and opportunity she'd been given.

The guilt that weighed on her heart about the car accident would pop its ugly head every once and awhile – no, daily - but it didn't consume her for the remainder of the day. She didn't think she would ever get over that dreadful night.

It was raining that night, more than the usual Florida storm. To her mother's dismay, Hope insisted on going to the local writers' symposium. It only occurred once a quarter and she missed the last time as a result of the flu. Her mother insisted on coming, as if her presence would only increase their safety in the rain. Her mother's instincts were right that night. They were returning, in the dark, with rain pouring from the sky in sheets. Hope was only able to see five inches in front of the glow of her headlights. She was cautiously driving below the posted speed limit, but that didn't prevent the car in the next lane from hydroplaning, over-correcting, and drifting straight into Hope and her mom's car.

When the car settled on the deep road ditch, the only sound Hope could hear was the blaring radio and the engine fighting to stay on. When Hope finally opened her eyes, she looked around at the shattered glass, and the acrid smell of smoke and fuel immediately filled her nose. She quickly assessed herself before frantically reaching over to the passenger seat. "Mom!" she cried. "Mom! Are you okay?" She shifted in her seat, the hot burning sensation in her side stopping her from moving much further. She craned her neck to look at her mom, her cries only echoed with silence. Once her eyes adjusted, she saw her mother's form slumped in her seat, the gravity on the incline pulling her body sideways, and her head to the side toward the decline. Her mouth pooled with blood and her skin was already a pale hue. She panicked. "MOM! Wake up! Please wake up!" Hope only then began to realize that the rain was pouring in through the broken windows.

Then she heard the voices. "Hello? Are you okay? Stay where you are! We've called 9-1-1." The voices were faint, drowned out by the rain, the engine, the radio, and her own sobs. All she could do was cry. It felt like an eternity but help did show up. She begged for the police officer to get her mother out first, but they insisted on rescuing her. They promised that the EMTs and firefighters were working on saving her mother. That evening was a blur. The ambulance, the sirens, the doctors, the nurses…her dad. It was her dad who told her. It was her dad who took her hand, and through his own pain and anguish, told her, "Mom is gone, she didn't make it, they did everything they could." The accident took only seconds to occur but it caused a lifetime of wounds.

Hope splashed her face with cold water, shaking herself out of her thoughts. She didn't want to relive that night. She was trying to escape it. She leaned back and reached for the stray blue towel and patted her face dry, then looked at herself again. The dark swollen circles remained, from the tears that still escaped at night, but the color in her cheeks was coming back. She stopped eating, working out, and in a true sense, functioning. She knew, deep down, her mother would never want her to grieve this way, but it was the only way Hope knew how to cope – to run away. It was slowly working, though.

Hope sighed and walked out of her room to peek at her cell phone. She wasn't expecting a call or a text, but it was a habit. A habit she still didn't break in the last six months. She had a large circle of friends before she ran away, and that was when she built the walls. People stopped calling and texting because she just stopped responding. To her surprise, there was a text. Dad.

Hi Sugar. How are you? You haven't called in a few weeks. Are you okay? I miss you. – Dad

A wave of fresh guilt washed over her. No, she hadn't called her dad. He lost Mom too, maybe a greater loss than her own. She hit the reply button.

Hi Dad. I love you. I am okay. Call you later?

She smiled softly; she did enjoy the fact that Dad signed off his texts as if she didn't know who it was from. She waited a moment before hitting the "Call" button, not waiting for a response. There wasn't a better time but now, and Hope knew it would make her dad's day to get her call.

She waited briefly before she heard that warm, low voice. "Hello? Sugar? Hope? Is that you? I was just going to write you back," her dad said, his sweet southern drawl coming out. It was clear he was thrilled to hear from her. Dad only called his girls "Sugar," and Hope enjoyed the term of endearment.

"Hi Dad, I'm sorry I haven't called. It's been kind of crazy at the Koffeehaus," she replied, a partial truth. Nothing special was happening but she did pull some extra shifts on the weekend to earn some extra money recently. "How are you doing? Everything alright?" she asked, hopeful. His voice sounded more like his old self than from recent conversations.

"I'm glad you're keeping busy. Everything is going as usual. Jack and I are heading to Fort Lauderdale for a bowling competition later this week. Everyone misses you, Hope. They always ask about you," her Dad added. Hope knew he wasn't lying, for the most part. It was a shock to everyone when she said she was leaving, and left within two days of her announcement. She couldn't take the pity anymore, the look in people's eyes when she walked into a store, or a friend's house. She needed to get away. Hope prayed daily that her Dad would understand, and he did. He never seemed to begrudge her. It was like he knew that she needed this space.

"Thank you, Dad. Say hi to everyone for me. Things are going well here. Mrs. Lulu's coffee place is busy, and she's taught me a lot." Her words were honest. She did enjoy her time here. Jacksonville was the home of Camp Lejeune, a United States Marine Corps Base. The city was filled with colorful people, especially the young men and women that escaped the base for a brief moment of civilian life. She enjoyed the banter, the grittiness at times of the servicemembers, but every individual she encountered loved coffee, and she was good with that. She shifted her focus off herself. "Dad, how is Harper doing? I haven't talked to her either. Is she doing better in school?" Her heart pained for her little sister, who struggled in school after Mom died, and struggled even more when she left. It wasn't fair. The guilt was overwhelming at times, but these were the consequences of her choices. She left a lot behind, and many people who wouldn't forgive her for now. She was blessed the most important people did: her dad and Harper.

"She's pulling through. I have her going to this counselor from church. She seems to like her. Her grades are coming up and she wanted to go to Lindsey's birthday thing the other day," Dad offered the promising news.

Hope smiled as if he could see her. "That *is* good, Dad! I'm glad things are looking better. You know, you can always call or text me. If you need anything, I'm here." Her voice was soft, trying not to break.

"I know, sugar. You can do the same thing. You do your thing. We are here. Harper wants to visit soon. Maybe you can give your ol' man a break from her teenage angst?" Dad chuckled, and Hope's heart warmed.

"Absolutely. I'd love for Harper *and you* to come visit. It's a tiny house, but you would really like it. There isn't much here in Jacksonville... bars, tattoo parlors, and a lot of smoke shops, but we can always drive a few minutes to the coast. We are closer to the beach here than in Jacksonville, Florida." Her voice was bright, hopeful for the future visit. Although she didn't want to come home, she would cherish seeing her dad and sister for a brief time.

"We would like that, Hope. So, maybe I could drop her off for a bit sometime this summer?" Dad offered, his own voice filled with a layer of happiness. "You guys could have a sisters' week or something."

"Definitely. When you know when you want to come, tell me, so I can let Lulu know when I need off." Hope sighed, content with how things were panning out. It was only a few months ago that their conversations were short, one-word answers and few-word questions. This conversation actually felt *normal*.

"I will, sugar. Call your sis sometime, okay? I know she'd be happy to hear from you," Dad suggested, rather intuitively.

"I promise, I will. I also promise to stay in better touch. Things are truly going well here, Dad. Everyone here is nice, and I think I'm finding my groove. I even got my guitar back from the music shop yesterday," Hope replied.

"Oh, that's great. You enjoy playing again then. There isn't anything more peaceful than being in the zone. I know that's where you go when you play." She could hear the smile in his voice, recollecting their conversations over guitar playing, singing, and even song writing.

"I plan to, Dad. I plan to." Her voice trailed off, nothing somber, just content.

"Okay, well, I need to get up off my ass and go to the grocery store this morning, or Harper and I won't be eating anytime soon. Talk to you soon, I hope?" Dad's voice was warm, and hopeful for another call soon.

"Absolutely, Dad. I promise. Give Harper a hug for me. I promise to call her before the weekend is up." Hope nodded into the phone, pulling the covers and sheets back in place, making her bed. "Talk to you later?"

"Have a good day. Remember, I love you always."

"I love you too, Dad." Dad hung up, and Hope set her phone down on the nightstand and pulled the remaining covers up and over her pillows. The day was already starting off well.

Once she was happy with how her room was picked up, she stepped out into the living area, and only a few paces into the kitchen. She needed to start a pot of coffee. Even after spending her whole week around coffee, she always enjoyed making her own pot at home.

According to Mrs. Lulu, Hope was bastardizing the process by using a standard kitchen drip coffee maker at home. Mrs. Lulu insisted on using a pour over method, where the water was brought to a certain temperature and then poured over in a specially-designed porcelain funnel, which then dripped into the mug or cup. Hope had to admit, she did enjoy the flavor that the pour over version created, but she didn't have the proper equipment, nor the patience to brew it this way at home. Mrs. Lulu would be dismayed. She smiled, thinking of her older woman friend.

Once Hope had her first cup of coffee, she leaned back against her counter, looking around the small perimeter of the kitchen. She needed to spruce this place up. Maybe some square paintings under the cupboards. Hope scanned the walls, planning and sketching her thoughts out. The kitchen was the next space she would "own." She pushed off the counter with her hip and made it over to the surface that had been baptized as the mail counter.

She sorted the pieces of mail, and only stopped when she got to the local coupon clipping magazine. The cover was a Marine, posed with a dog, clearly a pet. It was cute. She couldn't figure out what the advertisement was for, but her thoughts began to wander to Chad. She hummed softly to herself as she thought of him. He was always so playful, and flirty. She relished in his afternoon or evening coffee visit after he left base each weekday. He always seemed to brighten the end of the day.

Chad never spoke about another woman or partner. He would have if he had one, right? He did talk about his work, and his unit. She drummed her hands across the counter as she returned her attention to cleaning her kitchen. She supposed it was her turn to make things personal the next time they talked. She kicked herself most of the last few days since their conversation about writing. Their chats were always amusing, and light, but that one was particularly awkward. She tried not to share the shadowed parts of her life to him. She wanted to keep their talks bright, and he kept the last few conversations light and nothing deep after that one. Hope was convinced that she had turned him off, but he came back every day the rest of the week, so she must not have. Hopefully.

"Stop thinking about him, Hope," she muttered to herself as she wiped down the counters and began to polish the glass top stove. But only if she could. He was fit, handsome, and his broad shoulders in his shirt always stood out to her. She wanted to wrap herself around him. Chad was probably even more handsome in his uniform. Hope never saw him in it, but who would disagree though, that a man in uniform was attractive? She laughed to herself as she wandered around in her own fantasy. She wondered if Chad had a six-pack, and was pretty sure he did by how the rest of his body looked. He was trim too; not too much, of course.

Dang men and their metabolism, she thought. He used heaping tablespoons of sugar in his coffee, but still maintained that physique. She continued to laugh. He never had a bagel at the shop, he claimed there were too many carbs, and Hope planned to tease him the next time he turned down a bagel she offered.

As she finished wiping down the counters, sweeping the kitchen, and taking out the trash, she began humming that familiar tune. The tune she was trying to sharpen for the guitar. She wondered if Chad played an instrument. Music was the blood that ran through her veins, along with coffee. It's what made her heart beat in the morning. She enjoyed music as much as she enjoyed writing.

Writing. Oh, how Hope missed writing. The thoughts began to simmer, and wells of regret began to rise, but she quickly turned her thoughts back to Chad. He did mention being devoted to his job, and probably never spent time at home. Maybe he wasn't interested in being in a relationship? She never considered that. Chad never mentioned having any children, or pets, but she didn't have any of her own either. Chad most likely used the time they had together each day to decompress from base life. He probably even lived on base. Maybe he didn't? The weight of realizing how much she didn't know began to sink in. She didn't know his rank, but derived he was in a leadership position. Possibly an officer, but none of that weighed on her mind as important; just that he was in a state of perpetual stress.

It did occur to her, he would have to be deployed at some point. With the nature of the situation in some areas of the world, the military had been called upon heavily in the last two decades. She wondered if he faced those challenges - combat, war, deployment, being far away from home?

The military always complicated things. What was she doing, even letting that cross her mind? She wasn't capable of handling a relationship right now; at least, not in her mind. Hope didn't move away from everything she knew to look for a boyfriend. She needed to keep her mind clear. Anyway, Chad and Hope had been talking for over several months and he had never asked her out on a date. *Remember that, Hope*, she thought. *Remember that.* Maybe she should ask him? No, that would be way out of her comfort zone. Hope laughed at herself. She moved away to get out of her comfort zone, and the irony of it wasn't lost on her.

She moved on into the inner part of her home, cleaning and picking up things as she passed. She wasn't a slob, but it had been a few weekends since she vacuumed and did her laundry. It was time to dust as well, but Hope knew all of that could wait. The music store had taken a month to fix her guitar, and in all honesty, laundry and dusting could wait. With a small pep in her step, a refilled mug of coffee and her guitar in hand, she stepped out onto the front porch. She had never sat out here since she moved here, but playing her guitar was the perfect way to christen the porch.

chapter four

CHAD

*C*HAD PUSHED THE SHOWER CURTAIN back before he stepped out onto the bath mat. Damn, he needed that shower. It was a long week of mission evaluations and assessments. Too much bullshit for his own mind to absorb, so he took it out in the gym. He'd walked out of the gym this morning, dripping in sweat. He dished out all his frustration and anger in the weights he lifted, and in his run. Chad found solace when he trained. There was nothing more than focus and exertion during his weight training and honestly, that's what he needed. The paperwork and meetings were piling up, and the stress levels amongst his fellow officers and his unit members were rising. Their equipment was not being loaded fast enough and their safety checks weren't cleared yet. Deployment was less than nine months away and they needed to be much further along than they were. At least he had his run left for the day, right?

He wrapped a towel around his waist, and used a second one to dry his shoulders, chest, and then his head. He could go for a good cup of coffee right now, but he wasn't up for driving to Koffeehaus, knowing Hope wasn't there. Em was a sweet lady, but she wasn't Hope. He made that mistake once, but never openly admitted it. He did enjoy Koffeehaus's coffee, it was clean and crisp; but he enjoyed the company he kept while he was drinking it.

Hope, she was beautiful, there wasn't a question, but she was a puzzle he couldn't figure out. She never mentioned having a boyfriend, and she certainly wasn't wearing a wedding band. He enjoyed their banter and their conversation. It was a breath of fresh air after hours behind closed doors, and even more hours out in the field. Her eyes were bright, and she always offered a smile, even when he knew she was "off" that day. Why didn't he ask her out? He was a chicken, that's why. And when? And with what intention?

No woman in their right mind would want to date a man who was about to be deployed. The divorce and break-up rate in the Marine Corps was absurd, and he didn't ever want to join the ranks amongst his peers. He was certain Hope shared the same thoughts, although he never expected the woman to offer to go out; she never was so forward to even imply a date. Maybe she was just being polite. *No*, he thought. She was different with him. She always offered refills, and always sat down with him if she could. He never saw her do that with others, or maybe she did when he wasn't around.

Self-doubt was a man's worst enemy. It was something he had touted to his unit. Confidence in all actions was important. That is why they spent hours and days in the field practicing the same mission movements - for confidence. So, what was his hold-up in asking her out for dinner? It was just dinner, right? An evening as friends. He and Hope spoke daily during the week; it was a rarity to not see her, unless he was out in the field, but he never saw her outside of Koffeehaus. It was a pleasant surprise to see her instead of Mrs. LuLu during the week she moved in. Mrs. Lulu was a lovely person, but she wasn't Hope either.

Hope. That's it, he was going to ask her out for dinner; that was the plan.

He finished dressing, pulling his shirt over his head and running his hand through the the hair he had on top of his head. Today's plan was to lift weights, get a haircut, go for a run, get coffee, grocery shop, and laundry. Maybe in that order, maybe not. It was the weekend and Chad was just letting things flow. He looked around his bathroom and gathered the clothes that collected on the floor throughout the week. He carried the pile to the kitchen, where his washer and dryer were housed in a closet. Stuffing the clothing unceremoniously into the washer, he set the timer, added detergent, and then turned back to his kitchen. Coffee. He needed coffee. He joined the twenty-first century last year with an automated coffee machine. The aroma was wafting throughout the home, and his body was calling for it.

He pulled a large mug, shale gray, with the United States Marine Corps globe, eagle, and anchor. Chad was a Marine, through and through. There was references to the military, the USMC and all things USA, throughout his house. If there was such a place as a bachelor's pad, it was his home. He held the cup to his chest, taking in the aroma before shifting over to where he stored the sugar. He poured his sugar, as he thought of his typical cup of coffee during the week, poured by Hope, sweetened by himself, and then their enjoyable conversation. He did miss those exchanges on the weekend, but it made Monday afternoon coffee that much more special, at least for him.

He wondered what Hope was doing this weekend. In just the few months since they'd met, Hope rarely offered information about her life, even though they talked every day. She did mention she was new to Jacksonville, and that she was only just meeting people and settling into a routine, but she never talked about why she moved here. She was probably a socialite, hanging out with her new friends.

Chad had originally assumed that it was for a boyfriend, but he was certain now, for the most part, that Hope was not here for a man. She was here for a reason she didn't share with him. He was definitely going to be more bold. What was the worst that could happen? She could say no, but she still would have to pour his coffee every day. He chuckled, running his free hand across the top of his head and down his neck. Here he was, a Marine, stumbling over a woman! If his men knew how many times he questioned himself, he wouldn't live it down. He took the last swig of his coffee and set the cup in the sink.

Chad chose to get his run in early, even if it meant he was going to be super sore after his lifting session earlier and he had to take another shower soon after his first one. He wanted his coffee to be still in his system. Chad went into his room and slipped on his running socks, and grabbed his favorite Pittsburgh Penguins hat, and returned to the kitchen. He didn't plan the route in his head; he wanted to run just to clear his head. He ran most of the streets multiple times and knew his way back fairly quickly, but he was planning a little longer run today.

After grabbing a bottle of water, he stepped outside, locking the door and hiding the key under the gnome statue by the doorstep. He patted the gnome affectionately before he walked down the driveway, pausing at the mailbox to stretch briefly. Setting the water down to get into deeper stretches for his back, hamstrings, and quads, he debated what direction he would start. The sky was clear and brightening into a beautiful blue sky, and the neighborhood was quiet with little traffic this early in the morning.

Once his body was warmed up, he pushed off the driveway and started running. Those first few strides, and the first few miles, were always the hardest. Each stride reminded him he wasn't getting any younger, but with time, Chad found his rhythm and pace. His breathing was even with each stride.

Even with his mid-thirties body, running was automatic for Chad, especially after those first few miles. It came as natural as walking. Every training, every deployment, every day he could fathom working out, Chad ran. It cleared his mind, and left him rejuvenated for the rest of the day. The only thing he allowed his mind to register in his memory was the direction he was headed.

Chad nearly kicked himself for forgetting his earbuds on the front porch near the gnome statue. He now had to entertain himself visually, instead of pacing himself with his personal classic rock playlist. The neighborhood was filled with an eclectic group of homes. It wasn't like the new neighborhoods going up outside of Jacksonville, with only three or four different models on square pieces of land. Those houses were cookie cutter, with homes only changing in color or model. The houses in Chad's neighborhood each had their own look. Some homes looked their age of thirty or forty years, and others were clearly newly renovated. Some of the lawns were well-manicured with beautiful edging, while others were grown over with weeds. Chad preferred the well-manicured, yet aged, homes. He believed they had character. The walls of these homes have seen many days and nights. He enjoyed the creek of the wood floors in his own cottage-style home. Chad had the option of living on base since he was a bachelor, but he did that early on and learned quickly it was a much better option to escape the uniformed life at some point.

The sun rose above the roofline of the homes toward the east. He would occasionally lift a hand in a greeting when he recognized a car or family. Many of the homes here were rented by military families. He never fully could escape the military life, but it rarely bothered Chad. He leaned into the left curve as he paced his run down an unfamiliar neighborhood street. Chad scanned the homes to see the distinct uniqueness before his attention was drawn to a guitar strumming and a soft voice. The voice and guitar grew louder and louder as he moved further down the road.

It was a sweet song, one he didn't recognize, and it was a nice addition to the morning as the sun began to peek through the trees. He looked around, searching the porches for its source before he saw her. She was alone, seated on a chair, hugging the guitar to herself as if it were a part of her own body. It was clear she was proficient in playing. Her body was swaying to the rhythm.

He slowed his run down, trying not to make it obvious he was curious, but as he got closer, he began to notice the familiarity of the female form. Her blonde hair was pulled back in with clips to keep the strands out of her face. Her soft facial features - she was singing with her eyes closed - he appreciated an artist who felt their work. She had one leg tucked underneath herself casually, and was singing to herself. He smiled but then suddenly he blinked, and he realized why that female form was very familiar, just without an apron or coffee in hand. The singing artist was Hope. Hope lived in this neighborhood?

He slowed his run to a walk as he approached her driveway. Chad didn't want to interrupt her; he enjoyed seeing her in a different light. She was a beautiful woman, graceful in her movement. Chad appreciated the femininity Hope exuded. She wasn't a girlie girl, with fancy hair or makeup, but she exuded this graceful feminine vibe that drove his mind crazy. He started to walk up the driveway, hoping he wouldn't startle her.

He paused at the end of the walkway to her porch. "Good morning, Hope!" His breathing was still faster than typical but it was slowing down with his walking.

Hope dropped the leg she had tucked underneath herself when she opened her eyes, mildly startled by the unexpected greeting. Her cheeks flushed with color after she realized her audience was someone she knew. She smiled warmly - that smile he liked; the one that started at the edges of her eyes before it even started at her mouth. She waved.

"Hey Chad, what are you doing here?" Her voice was filled with surprise.

Chad invited himself up the walkway and to the steps of the front porch. He stopped at the second step, leaning against one of the entry way pillars. "I was going to say the same thing but realized I was at your home, not vice versa. I live about five streets west of here, closer to the entrance to our neighborhood. I've never run down this particular road before." He paused and smiled at her, resting a hand on his hip. "I may have done it more often if I knew you lived here," he flirted with a soft chuckle.

Hope's cheeks filled with a crimson color again; he

loved watching her blush. "Well, it wasn't like it was public knowledge." She laughed. "I wouldn't mind watching you run up and down the street. You're better eye candy than most of my neighbors." She returned the flirtation, while gingerly leaning her guitar against the wall of the front porch.

Chad patted his chest. "Well that makes me proud, I think," he jested. "How long have you been playing guitar? I never knew you could play and sing."

Hope smiled up at him, before glancing down at her beloved instrument. "Oh, I learned when I was a kid. It came naturally, I suppose. I just got her back from the music store. She sustained some damage in the move. They fixed her back up and I thought I'd spend my morning breaking her new strings in." She reached down to run her fingers across the rim of the guitar fondly.

"You are really talented. Why don't you play at the Koffeehaus sometime? It'd drum up some business and you'll get to play more often," he suggested as he leaned his head against the pillar. He admired the way she delicately touched her instrument; he too knew that love. He hadn't played in years, and he missed it. He admired her gentle touch on the surface of her guitar. It was that feminine quality she had. His mind wandered for a brief moment, imagining how her hands would feel on his skin, but he quickly returned his attention to the proper source.

"Nah, I don't usually play for crowds. It's just a hobby," Hope mused. "Do you want to sit? I can grab another chair from inside, even get you a cup of coffee. It's free today, you know," Hope teased as she stood up to make her way inside.

The tank top and cotton shorts she wore hugged her small, but curvy form. Chad rarely got to see Hope without a matronly apron on, but he always admired her figure. She had the perfect hourglass shape in a small, delicate package.

He responded quickly, "No...no need for a chair, I can sit on the step. But I'll gladly take one of your free cups of coffee today." Chad smiled as he lowered himself onto the step, bending a knee to his chest. "You do have sugar, right?" He winked at her.

Hope opened her screen door as she stepped in, quipping at him when he winked, "What if I said I didn't?" Her smile was bright today. It had to be because she wasn't at work or stressed, and Chad was glad to have her undivided attention.

"Well, I'd have to drink the coffee black, then. Trust me, I've had my share of black coffee on base. The shit that grows hair on your chest," Chad remarked, his mouth curled in distaste, remembering all the coffee he and his counterparts ingested during meetings, mission briefings, and trainings.

"I'm kidding, of course. I'll make sure to bring some out so you don't become more of a hirsute man." She laughed, shaking her head and letting the screen door close behind her with a light tap.

Chad smiled, laying an arm across his knee, looking out into the front lawn. His run was derailed, but he didn't care. This was the best distraction of his day. He looked at her lawn and tilted his head, noticing it needed some work. It didn't look bad, but it needed some sprucing. He would ask her if she needed help, mowing her lawn and helping her out, perhaps for extra time with her. Chad turned to look toward the door when he heard the old springs creak.

He quickly stood up to take the steaming cup of coffee from her. She had tucked a glass sugar dispenser under her arm with a small spoon in her other hand. Sitting back down, Chad gingerly placed the mug on the porch floor, then took the sugar and spoon from Hope. "Thank you. I never intended to interrupt your jam session." He smiled up at her as she sat in her white wooden chair, while he poured the sugar into the hot coffee.

Hope almost choked on her refilled cup of coffee. She covered her mouth, laughing. "I wouldn't call what I was doing a jam session and I don't mind taking a coffee break. It's a pleasant surprise, actually. You said you lived here, too? West?" She motioned toward the homes around them.

Chad stirred his coffee. "Yeah, I live off Acosta Street. It's a two-bedroom, cottage-style house. It's small, and old, but I love it." He brought the cup up to his lips, blowing softly before sipping.

Hope smiled, looking at him as she sipped from her own cup. "I like the quaintness of the neighborhood. It isn't pretentious." She tucked a stray hair behind her ear. His heart fluttered watching her do that. "This is Mrs. Lulu's house too. When she found out I was looking for a place after hiring me, she insisted that I move in here. She really is my angel."

Chad nodded. "Lulu is a sweet soul. She has a way with her customers, though. If she doesn't like you, you know it. Lulu knows her coffee too. One time, I made the mistake of asking her what the difference was between the different brews. I didn't think I would ever get out of there." He laughed at the tongue-in-cheek joke. A comfortable silence surrounded them, and Chad looked up at the roof of the porch and then back down to her. "So, this is what you do on the weekend, huh? Drink coffee and play your guitar," he mused, resting the mug on his knee, leaning his head back on the wood surface.

Hope offered a small huff and rolled her eyes. "You make it sounds so glamorous. Yes, I'm pretty laid back. I have a tendency to do some reading too, if I don't pick up an extra shift at Koffeehaus."

"You already work during the week, why work during the weekend?" he asked, surprised.

Hope smiled. "More work equals more money. The move here was kind of sudden, so I sort of accrued some debt I want to pay off. In fact, I think I'll be done paying all that off by my next check." She nodded, clearly proud of her hard work.

"Wow, that's awesome! Not a lot of people could say they actively try to pay off their debt nowadays. They just sorta let that shit grow," he commended her. Her body language was comfortable; the last thing he wanted to do was to make her feel awkward. "When I joined the military after college, I sort of lost control. I saw a paycheck twice a month and thought I was rich. It took some deployment money to pay that shit down. Lesson learned, that's for sure." He lifted his mug to toast her achievement.

"I'm curious, can I ask you a question?" Hope curled her legs up underneath her.

Chad nodded, glad she was interested in him. "Sure. Shoot."

Hope tilted her head holding her mug to her torso. "How long have you been in the military?"

Chad smiled. "I joined when I was 20, after I graduated from college with a degree in business management. This will be my sixteenth year." He cringed. "I feel old. Fuck, I never knew I'd even get this close to 20 years."

Hope took a sip from her cup. "That's a huge commitment. What made you want to join?"

"Ah, well, I was young, rebellious, and I wanted to see

the world. My dad was a Marine during Vietnam, and my Grandfather was a Marine in World War II, so I figured I'd carve my way into the legacy while seeing the world." She listened intently, and he continued, "I have seen some pretty fucking awesome places, but damn, have I seen some of the shittiest places on Earth." He pondered for a moment, before adding, "Probably not the shittiest places...more like, places inhabited by some shitty people."

"Oh." Hope was absorbed in the conversation, his crass language never affecting her. "You said you were deployed. Did you see combat? How many times did you have to go?" She spoke with a genuine curiosity that only encouraged Chad to answer.

"Early on in my career, I was attached to a bunch of different units that deployed and saw combat. As a young officer, I was out in the field with my guys, so yeah, I saw some, I had to pull the trigger. But my direct job wasn't specific to infantry, even though I have units now that are combat ready to be deployed against any enemy. As I've gotten promoted, I've moved closer and closer inside the wire and less outside. The only time I really am out in the field is when we are in transport or doing final inspections as a unit. I've been deployed five times since I joined." He shook his head, waving his hand at her. "You really didn't need to know all that military mumbo jumbo."

Hope rested her mug on her thigh as she listened. "That sounds super scary." She paused. "But I did ask you the question, you know." Chad's heart warmed when he saw Hope wink at him.

"Yes, yes you did." He grinned. "Yeah, there were some scary moments. I never wanted to lose a guy, ever. I knew my orders, even if they weren't my direct orders, put each of those men or women in direct threat when we were deployed. There have been times where we would lose contact or a mission wouldn't go as planned. Those are the moments, I think, that make me question what the fuck I'm doing, and then I have to try to see the greater goal. As a leader, I need to be there, in the good, the bad, and the ugly. It doesn't mean that it doesn't affect me." He took a deep breath, drawing in a long swallow of coffee. He shook his head at the stress rising in him. "Enough military, though; it really isn't as interesting as it sounds." He paused to redirect the conversation. "So, since you asked me some questions, may I ask you some?"

Hope smiled, "Sure. I appreciate you sharing too. It can't always be that easy." She leaned back, as if she was preparing to take on a barrage of questions.

"No, no it's not, but I wouldn't change anything about my career. I've met some of the most incredible men and women doing what I do. Definitely wouldn't change it." He held the warm mug to his chest, his fingers of one of his hands tapping while he thought. "So, what do I want to know about Hope…." He mused for a moment. "I've been dying to know, what brought you to this shithole, of all places. It's not like you're connected to the military, or are you?"

Hope laughed at his description of the city, before responding, "Well. To be brutally honest, I was running away." Her voice was quiet, somber, but she continued, even though every line on her face proved she was hesitating. "My mom and I were in a car accident about nine months ago. I wanted to go to a writing symposium, and it was pouring outside. She insisted I not go, but I, being stubborn, insisted on going. She decided to join me, thinking it would make me safer. No matter how slow I was going, I couldn't get the car out of the way of the truck that hit us. He hydroplaned and crossed two lanes." She took a swallow of her coffee, as if she was clearing her mouth of the experience. "I had some minor stuff, but my mom…" The words were barely audible. "My mom." She stalled at the end of her statement. She looked down at her coffee. "She didn't make it." She took another pause, the wrinkles forming deeper over her brows as she stared into her coffee. "My mom was my best friend. She did everything with me. She supported everything I ever did. After she died, I couldn't handle the looks, the words, the way people treated me. It made me sick. I blamed myself." She looked up at him, her eyes filled with tears. "I still blame myself for losing our mom. I should've listened and stayed home, but I insisted. I was selfish. I wanted to hear the speakers that night. It didn't matter that the roads were treacherous from the rain. I figured it was another bipolar Florida weather day." Hope's words trailed for a moment, before ending in silence.

Chad sat in the silence, surprised at how forthcoming she was, and deeply moved by her answer. He leaned his head on the wood, shaking his head before replying very softly, "It wasn't your fault, Hope." That is all that Chad could summon as an offer in comfort. He closed his eyes for a moment, before opening them when he heard her reply.

"I know." Hope hugged her mug against her lower abdomen and legs. "That's why I moved to Jacksonville." She paused, her tone of voice changing to one of mild amusement. "I'm from Jacksonville, Florida, and just randomly looked for another Jacksonville in the United States. This one was close enough to go home to my dad or sister quickly, but far enough to run away and avoid it all." She looked at him, biting her lower lip before finishing, "I researched some places to work, and contacted Mrs. Lulu when I saw her 'help wanted' ad. She and I hit it off from the first phone conversation, and I moved a few days after that." The conversation didn't grow awkward; it was somber, but natural. They were both sharing a bit about themselves. Vulnerability is a good foundation for a friendship.

"Well shit, Hope. I'm really sorry." Chad mentally kicked himself. He was terrible about offering sympathetic words. It really wasn't his strong suit. "Well, at least you landed a pretty good gig at Lulu's." He took a deep breath, realizing the weight of the conversation had made him hold his breath. "Are you doing okay here? Is Jacksonville, North Carolina all you imagined it would be?" He smirked, trying to lighten the mood.

Hope offered a small smile at his joke. "It's everything I ever dreamed of." Her remark was sarcastic, but the levity was welcomed by both parties. "I didn't expect to see so many tattoo parlors, but you know, you Marines and your tattoos," she quipped, hiding her brighter smile behind her mug.

Chad laughed at her jab. "Yeah, we tend to enjoy a bit of ink on our skin. I'm glad you're adjusting alright." He paused, allowing the silence to grow between them. As hard as the conversation was, it was comfortable, and not forced. They were good with silence, he noticed. He enjoyed her company far more than he ever expected. He took the last swig from his mug before setting it down on the porch floor. He looked at his watch, shaking his head, having never reset his timer for his run, and he realized how long he had lingered. He looked up at her, contemplating the idea he had in mind. "Hope?"

She opened her eyes from her own contemplative state

during the silence. "Hmm?" She sipped her coffee delicately, waiting for his reply.

He stood up slowly, bringing his cup with him. "So... I have an idea." He paused, watching her for any clues she may say no. "How about I finish this run, and then come by in an hour or two and pick you up for lunch? Now that I know where you live and all." His smile crinkled the corners of his eyes as he teased. "We can finish our conversation then?" He cocked his head, eagerly awaiting a response.

Hope lowered her mug and stood when he did. She was a bit surprised at first, and let the question linger in the morning air for a bit before responding. "Sure, Chad, I'd really like that." Her smile lit her whole face.

Fuck, she was gorgeous right then, standing in front of him. The way the tank top clung to her chest, outlining her curves, made his breath catch. He had to reign in his reaction or he may run into some trouble holding back. All he wanted to do was place his hands on her beautiful face and kiss her, but that would ruin this moment for sure. "Great. I'll see you at noon? Wear something comfortable, I'll take you to my favorite pizza place in town and show you some places you can explore." He handed his mug to her, her fingers brushing his. Chad's heart skipped a beat as he made his way down the stairs. He was certainly going to need a cold shower when he returned home.

"Great. I'll be ready by then. Thank you, Chad. You really don't have to, you know." She stood at the top of the stairs as he made his way down the walkway.

"I know." Chad turned to look at her. "I want to, though," he replied, his grin showing the honesty in his statement. "See you soon then?"

"See you soon, Chad. Thank you for stopping by."

Hope smiled, her body leaning on the front porch beam, an arm wrapped around it. She waved happily as she watched him make his way down the street.

Chad waved back and started a slow jog home. *Shit, Chad, you just invited her out on a date and she said yes. Don't screw this up.* His run seemed to end much quicker than typical for the distance he just ran, but he wasn't going to complain. He had a date with Hope.

He grinned as he unlocked the front door and pushed it open. He was going to take a woman out on a date. This was a first in several years. Dropping his keys on the counter, he began to strip off his clothing as he made his way to his room. Yes, a cold shower was what he was going to need to get his mind in the right place.

chapter *five*

HOPE

A DATE. CHAD JUST ASKED her on a date. She closed the door and pressed her back to it, squeezing her eyes shut. Her heart was racing as the reality of the situation sunk in. A smile spread across her face and she bit her lower lip. All those signs, and flirtatious come backs...he really was interested. This was certainly a shift in moods. For the first time in quite some time, Hope was excited.

Hope set the mugs and spoon she was holding into the sink and placed the sugar dispenser back in her cupboard. She paused once again, tapping her fingers on the counter. She looked at the digital clock on the stove. There was only an hour and half to figure out what she was going to wear and get ready.

Hope's cheeks almost ached from the grin she wore. She skipped into her room to sort through her closet. This was the first time since she moved that she needed to be intentional about what she was wearing. She knew exactly which outfit she was going to wear.

She sighed, walking into her small walk-in closet, flicking the light on. Her eyes searched the selection. She hadn't looked at these clothes since she moved in. She smiled brightly to herself as she pulled the outfit she was looking for from the hanger. This was it. It was an off-shoulder poet sleeve black romper with a gathered waist. It was one of her favorite outfits to wear when she went out with her friends. A perfect casual look but one that could be dressed up if she wanted.

Hope placed the romper on the edge of her bed as she gathered the other items she needed for the final *look*. She moved to her dresser and pulled out a pair of panties and matching bra, and tossed them on her bed.

She made her way to the shower, pulling her clothes off swiftly. Hope spent too much time looking for the right shirt. Stepping in the shower and pulling the curtain behind her, this shower had to be a quick one. When she was finished, she covered up with a towel, tucking the edge under her arm.

Hope took her time and got ready. She picked the nude-colored laced bra and panty set because they always made her more confident. Whenever she did a pitch at writing symposiums or conferences, she always wore this set. Hope ran her fingers over the fabric, smiling. The memories stung, but they were good memories. Pulling her favorite romper on, Hope was beginning to feel nervous.

Was she leading Chad on? Was she even prepared for a relationship? She didn't move to Jacksonville to find a relationship. Had she lost her mind? She shook her head as she pulled the towel off her head. She walked back into her bathroom, ducking to search the cabinet underneath the sink, finding her hair dryer, a beauty tool she hadn't used since she moved here. She had thick blonde hair, and it always took longer than she wanted.

She ran her hand through her hair after it was dried,

making sure the product held the way she wanted. Hope wasn't trying to get fancy; she wasn't really talented in that area. Her goal was to just look presentable. She leaned over the sink as she started putting on her makeup, debating on what or how much to put on. *It's lunch. Don't think too much, Hope, don't think too much. He has seen you in your apron, for God's sake.* She settled on a subtle natural look with plain gloss, no tint.

Satisfied with her makeup and hair, Hope walked to her door and sorted through the stack of shoes she kept near the entrance. She found the copper colored flip flops she wore to glam-up the outfit. She scanned across the counter surface, searching for her wristlet wallet. It was the glint of the metal zipper that caught her eye. She lifted it off the coffee table, opening it to make sure she had everything she needed.

Just like the disciplined Marine he was, Chad arrived on time. When she heard the doorbell, she opened the door, greeting his friendly face. That smile warmed her from the inside. He had a way of looking at her that made her feel like jell-o on the inside, making her stumble over her words. "Well, hello." Chad had showered and put on a fitted camo green t-shirt with jeans, something different than what she typically saw him in. "You look real nice." She smiled as she stepped outside, locking the door.

"You stole my line, Hope," he bantered. "You look very nice. I said we were just going for pizza." Chad laughed, offering his elbow like a gentleman, before moving down the front steps.

Hope happily took his arm, smiling warmly up at him. "Well, my apron is back inside if you want me to go get it." Her smile turned into a grin.

His head tilted back as he laughed. "No, no, I'll see you

in it soon enough." He walked Hope to the passenger side of his silver truck. His chivalry was endearing, and she wasn't surprised he did this. Hope held Chad's arm as she hoisted herself into the truck and she watched him as he crossed the front of the truck to his side, sliding in naturally. The car smelled like old leather, mixed with Chad's choice of deodorant or aftershave; Hope couldn't place it.

Hope buckled her seatbelt and leaned back against the seat. "My dad would like this truck," she remarked nostalgically.

"Oh? This piece of shit?" he joked, patting the dashboard fondly. "I kid. She's been good to me. We've been through many a duty station and deployment. I'm rather fond of her myself. What does your dad drive now?"

"A red, 1995 Ford F-150. He refuses to turn it in, but he idolizes the newer trucks." Hope smiled over at Chad as she talked about her father.

"Well, when he does decide to upgrade, he's going to be floored by all the technology." He leaned back, and placed his hand on the head of the passenger seat as he looked behind him. Hope noticed he didn't use the backup camera on his console.

She muffled a soft snicker, especially after his last remark. "Why don't you use your camera?"

He smiled, looking at her before changing gears and pressing forward through the neighborhood. "I don't think I'll ever trust a camera over my own two eyes. Unless, they're night vision goggles out in the desert. The camera doesn't cover the whole visual field. What if grandma crossed my path before the camera picked up on her? I'd crush her old self," he jested.

Hope shook her head, amused. "Well, I guess we wouldn't want to run over grandma, now would we?" She looked out the window as they drove through town, recognizing most of the byways and intersections they passed, but then he turned off a road she wasn't familiar with. "Where are we going again?"

He smiled at her. "Luigi's." He pointed to a shopping strip about a quarter mile ahead of them. "It's a locally-owned place, and they make the best pizza in this city. They're huge and fucking fantastic." He clearly liked his pizza, Hope thought. Hope enjoyed pizza too, and figured he probably knew what he was talking about.

"Good, because I am starving." She patted her stomach. "All that coffee this morning made my metabolism fire up." She winked at him, grinning again.

"Well, good thing we're close." He smiled back at her as he turned the truck into a long shopping strip, maneuvering into a parking spot. "Are you ready for the best pizza around here?"

"Absolutely. I'm looking forward to seeing what you call the best. Who knows, I may not like it." She unclipped her seatbelt and reached for her door handle.

"No." He touched her arm. "Let me." He slipped out of the truck and scurried to her side to open her door.

She smiled. "Well, that was gentlemanly of you." She touched his arm appreciatively as she slid down from the truck, her body grazing his. She noticed the hardness of his muscles, and the masculine woodsy smell he wore. Hope smiled, her cheeks blushing mildly as she admired him. She wasn't sure if he noticed, like she did. He had no response for her appreciation but a small smile, and a glint in his eye. Did he feel what she felt? Her cheeks burned hotter, and she smiled brighter as well. He closed the door behind her, pausing for a moment before he placed his hand on the small of her back, gently guiding her toward the pizza establishment. Her skin under his hand tingled and she became very aware of his touch. She held her breath to try to gain poise.

When they reached the entrance, he stepped ahead and opened the glass door, allowing her to enter. She stepped in, pausing to walk in with him, and he returned his hand to her back as they walked in together. He raised his other hand when he recognized the cook behind the checkered counter. "Hey Leo. Grab any table?" he inquired. After getting an affirmative thumbs-up, he casually grabbed two plastic menus and guided Hope to a corner booth, with a window view.

Chad stood by the booth, facing the door, leaving her to choose to sit next to him or across. She figured it is easier to talk with someone face to face and slid into the booth across from him. He sat as well, sliding the menu across the table. "Do you want to share a pizza? Get pizza by the slice?" he asked as he flipped through the menu, knowingly, familiar with the items of the menu. "Appetizer?"

Hope laughed. "Woooaaah there. Let me look at the menu." He nodded, chuckling, and she could tell he was mildly embarrassed with a hint of nervousness. Hope scanned the menu, feeling Chad's gaze on her. She pretended not to notice, but she was wondering what he was thinking. When she looked at Chad in moments like these, she could almost see wheels turning in his head; she knew he was thinking but it wasn't clear what about. Hope aspired to be able to read that quizzical gaze one day. "Well, there is so much here. What do you suggest? I'm not picky. I just don't like pineapple on my pizza." Hope raised her gaze to meet his.

He looked as though her eyes meeting his startled him,

and he blinked before he shuffled the menu back in his hands, scanning it. "Well." The weight of her last statement about pineapple finally occurred to him and his delayed laugh caused Hope to laugh as well. "Pineapple on pizza is a sin. Pizza debauchery at its worst."

Hope's eyes danced with amusement at his response. "I didn't realize pizza had free will."

He shook his head, still laughing. "It's not the pizza that has free will, it's the person who has the nerve to add pineapple to their pizza," he joked back. "How about we share a pepperoni with some of their garlic rolls?" Chad offered, the beguilement not leaving his eyes.

"Sure! That sounds good. I love pepperoni," Hope replied, sliding her menu to the edge of the table.

"What would you like to drink?" He slid out of the plastic booth, grabbing the menus.

"What do they have on tap?" Hope craned her neck to look at the counter behind her, hoping she wasn't choosing to drink too early, let alone on the first date.

"My kind of girl. Pizza and beer should be married, always." Chad grinned at her. "They have the usual, Corona and Bud, but can I get you one of my favorites as a surprise? I'll drink it if you hate it," he offered eagerly as he stood in front of her.

His proximity caught Hope off guard again. She inhaled sharply, her eyes followed his masculine outline, starting at his hips, right at her eye level, and moving upwards, the clothing clinging to a well fit body, making Hope pause to admire. Hope saw the definition in his forearm and his bicep as it peeked from underneath the sleeve of his polo shirt. She always enjoyed a man with good arms and abs.

"I can always just pick up a Bud or something..."

Chad broke Hope's silence and observation, an amused but puzzled look on his face.

"Oh… no, no, just get me your favorite, I'd love to try it." Hope blushed, shaking her head, waving her hand in the air as if she was brushing the awkward silence off.

Chad chuckled and nodded as he made his way to the counter. Hope could swear she saw him shake his head and she hoped she didn't embarrass herself too much. Did he mention the beer he liked? She was too distracted. Hope admonished herself for the goof, and not even offering to pay.

Hope smiled at him when he returned to the table with two bottles of beer and two cold mugs. The label read 'Black Dog Ale'. He'd chosen a red amber beer, which was new to Hope. She picked up the cold bottle and examined the label. "This looks interesting. I've never heard of it."

"I hadn't either. One of the guys on base introduced me to it and it's my go-to if restaurants carry it. It's got a sweet malt taste, but enough hop to take it through," Chad said confidently. It was clear he enjoyed his beer.

"Well, that was definitely far more technical than I know beer." Hope laughed, setting the bottle down. "But… I can certainly pour the proper beer," she offered with a grin.

"Oh, really? I'd be honored," Chad, intrigued, pushed his bottle and mug toward her as well.

Hope lifted his mug and angled the bottle, pouring the reddish amber liquid into the mug, ensuring the foam, or "head" as her father taught her, did not grow too much as the liquid flowed. She turned the mug upright to top off the bottle and allow the head to form. When about three-quarter inch head formed at the top, she pushed the mug over back to Chad. "Tada!"

"Wow. Look at that, not too much foam. Were you a server or a bartender in Florida?" Chad cocked his head to the side to examine his mug, nodding in approval before sliding his fingers into the mug's handle. His fingers were rugged, but clean and manicured, Hope noticed.

Hope laughed at the suggestion. "No, my parents wouldn't let me work in the food industry. My father is a big beer fan, so he taught me and my sister how to pour his beer when we were young."

"Boy, he should be proud," Chad chuckled, nodding to hers. "Pour your own; we need to toast."

Before his sentence was finished, Hope was pouring her own mug of beer, placing the empty bottle confidently on the table, smiling at Chad over her mug. "You said toast?" She lifted her mug up to initiate the tradition.

Hope loved the way Chad's eyes twinkled as he met her glass with his own. "Yes, a toast. A toast to beer and pizza. Forever married."

Hope laughed, repeating the same. "To beer and pizza." She nodded as she tapped her glass to his and brought it to her lips to try the beer for the first time, letting the taste simmer. Hope avoided looking at Chad while doing this, because she knew he was waiting for her assessment. But for a split second, her eyes met his and she nearly spit out the beer at his facial expression. She covered her mouth with her hand, swallowing before she asked, "Are you okay?"

Chad's eyebrows were elevated and his face was concerned. "I have a lot weighing on whether or not you like this beer. We just can't be friends if you don't like Big Dog Ale." Chad's expression broke before laughing.

Hope shook her head, "Well, no pressure then." She took a second sip, drinking much faster this time, shaking her head side to side, and then nodding. "Not bad. It's definitely sweeter than I am used to, but it's a good match with pizza. I approve." Hope paused. "So… can we still be friends?"

"You bet! You like beer with pizza and you like Black Dog Ale. It's win-win all around!" Chad winked at her and slid out of the booth and headed up to the counter to grab their order. *That wink.* Her heart fluttered, she clutched her shirt, chiding herself again. *You've been talking to this man for months; this is pizza and a beer.* But that wink? She bit her lower lip, only distracted by his return and the wafting aroma of pizza.

"Wow, this looks great. I'm starving!" Hope rubbed her hands together dramatically.

"Well, let's eat!" Chad smiled at her exclamation and passed her a paper plate. "Mind if I do the honors?"

"Please!" Hope agreed, settling back into her booth. Chad pulled a piece of pizza, first for her and then one for himself. After allowing the pizza to cool, they separately, without the cue of the other, dabbed their pizza with a napkin. Hope and Chad laughed when they noticed the unison of their action. The conversation flowed as they ate, simply enjoying the moment. Hope was having a difficult time reining in her emotions for Chad.

Chad was kind, yet she could tell there was an underlying masculine protectiveness. He was soft but built like a fighter. Her heart fluttered at her own thoughts, all while trying to keep track of their conversation. She learned he was a newly promoted lieutenant colonel in charge of several hundred men and women. It was clear why he always seemed stressed when he came for coffee. Hope also learned that he had never married, and didn't have any children. He said it again, that he was married to the

Corps, but he would like to find his partner for life. Hope noticed the sweet smile he had when he talked about that. *Duly noted*, she thought.

When both Hope and Chad couldn't eat any more, they sat back and looked at each other, grinning. "So? What'd you think?" Chad asked eagerly as he gathered their trash on the tray. "Want to take the leftovers?" He waved at the four generous slices that remained.

Hope laughed heartily, sticking her hand out, shaking her head. "No, I really shouldn't." She leaned over and helped him gather the trash together.

"How about we share the leftovers, then? Hmm?" he offered again as he stood to take the tray away.

"Sure, we can do that." She smiled up at him warmly, letting her hand brush against his. She felt the butterflies growing as she touched him, and wondered if he felt the same way? His face never gave it away. Chad returned to the table with two small boxes for the pizza, and Hope insisted on packing the leftovers. She batted at his hands playfully. "Let me do the packing, at least. You've done everything today."

He played coy and raised his hands innocently. "Okay, okay. I know I've done *so* much, getting pizza and beer today," he jested as he sat down to watch her pack up their leftovers.

"Well, thank you, Chad. The pizza was fantastic. I really appreciate it." She beamed at him, hoping her blush had died down.

"My pleasure, and I agree. The pizza was great. The company wasn't bad either," he teased, winking, as he took one of the packed boxes. "Should we head out?"

"Sure." She grabbed her box, and they walked toward the exit. Chad graciously held the door for her and as they approached his truck, he reached for the handle, holding her door open as she slid into the passenger seat.

"Here, let me hold that for you," Hope offered, holding her hand out for his box. Their hands touched again, and again Hope's heart felt the same familiar flutter. *Tame yourself.*

On their drive through town, Chad talked about all the places he thought she should explore, if she wanted to. In reality, Hope was wishing he would extend their afternoon as long as he could. She was enjoying his company, and it had been a very long time since she sat back and laughed, from the bottom of her soul, although his jokes were cheesy. She was enjoying his flirtations, and she truly didn't want this afternoon to end.

Chad drove Hope across what seemed to be the whole city. He quipped about different bars, the strip clubs and tattoo parlors, always claiming he had never been, but heard through others. Hope always felt the need to tease back.

After showing Hope the local park with a trail she could walk, he parked the car in front of a lake and sat back, looking at her. "I really like this lake," he said. "It has lily pads and lots of neat looking birds at random times of the year. I'm sure it's a migration thing, but it's a great place to visit too," he explained, while Hope listened, looking at their scenery fondly.

"It really is beautiful, peaceful. Maybe a picnic one day?" she asked, smiling back at him as they enjoyed the moment together.

"Absolutely! Let's get out, I'll show you my favorite spot," Chad offered, opening his truck door and jumping out.

Hope unlatched her door and stepped out, smiling,

enjoying the fact that Chad wanted to share a part of himself on their first date. As she walked around the front of the truck, he met her there and gingerly wrapped his arm around her lower back and waist. Hope leaned into the affectionate embrace. He felt right, he felt perfect.

Hope felt Chad turn her to him, his arm holding her body close. She pressed a hand against his chest, smiling up at him. His face hovered so close to hers, and she felt his warm, minty breath against her face. They lingered there in front of the lake for a little longer before he broke the silence.

"How about we grab some ice cream before heading back?" he asked, a hopeful glint in his eye.

Hope's heart was elated, knowing he wanted to extend the afternoon as well. "Please, I'd really like that, but I want to treat." She smiled teasingly, as they broke their embrace and made their way back to the truck. Hope hoisted herself into the truck when he opened her door for her. She watched him jog over to his side to slide into the driver side.

Chad feigned sulking as he turned the truck on. "No. First date, I treat," he insisted as he put the truck in reverse to enter the byway again.

"Fine, but your coffee is on me this week." Hope laughed, shaking her head at his gentlemanly insistence to pay for everything.

"Deal. I won't say no to that." Chad peeked over at her with that smile, the one that made her melt into her seat.

"Deal," she repeated, praying her voice wouldn't crack or give her emotions away. She watched out the window, balancing the pizza boxes in her lap. He knew the town like the back of his hand, and it was clear he left base a lot more often than she thought. Every few minutes, they would discuss a new location they would pass, or he would give his opinion about a certain store.

Hope sneaked a glance, admiring the way Chad drove his truck. He nearly hugged the wheel of his truck when he talked and drove, talking with his hands and his body. It was another endearing trait, and she tried to imagine him talking to the people he led. He was probably passionate, and she wondered if he was a hardass. She turned to look out the window, smiling at the thought of Chad being a hardass.

Chad pulled into the parking lot that held the simple soft serve ice cream booth. Chad turned to her and smiled. "Stay here and I'll bring it back. It's soft serve, but it's really good. They have the usual flavors, and things like cookies 'n creme, mint chocolate chip, and some peanut butter ones. Do you have a preference on flavor?" Chad slid out of his seat and faced her while standing in front of the driver side door.

Hope smiled at his eagerness, "Would it be terrible if I asked if they had any coffee-flavored versions?"

Chad shook his head, laughing. "No, it wouldn't be terrible; it'd be predictable, though. But yes, they do. That's actually my favorite, with chocolate chips mixed in. Want to try it? I didn't fail you on the beer."

Hope gave him a thumbs up. "No, you really didn't. That sounds great. Let's do it!" She grinned back at him as he left and watched as he jogged up the curb. *God, that back!* She noted the muscles flexing as he moved, and allowed herself to dive into her fantasy for a moment as he ordered. She watched him lean over, catching a peek of his arms. Was that a tattoo? She never noticed if he had any tattoos. If he did, he did a good job covering them. She made a mental note to ask.

When he approached the truck, a cup of ice cream in each hand, Hope returned her focus to the pizza boxes in her lap to ensure there was no spillage in his truck. Chad set a cup on the hood of the truck as he pulled his door open, leaning through the opening to hand Hope the second cup. It was filled to the brim, with a cone sticking out of the top, and Hope felt her mouth begin to water. Chad looked proud at her reaction. He grabbed his similarly decorated cup before sliding into his seat, and looked at her, anticipating her reaction. Chad lifted his cup up. "To coffee-flavored soft serve with chocolate chips?" he toasted with a hesitant questioning end.

Hope laughed, lifting her own cup before her first bite. "To coffee-flavored soft serve with chocolate chips," she repeated, and shook her head as she dipped into the sugared heaven. For several minutes, there was silence between them; the kind where the flavor was being savored and occasionally, a few grunts and "mmms" could be heard. Hope finally broke the silence between the crunch of her cone. "So, Chad, what's your favorite color?"

Chad chuckled, probably at the particularly random question. "Dark blue, but not that dark blue that looks black blue; that deep blue before it's considered 'navy' blue." He described the color very precisely. Hope found his need for detail intriguing, as she never really met a man that focused on detail. "What about you?"

"Dark pink. Nothing special about dark pink, just dark pink," Hope replied, teasing him for his detailed response.

Chad only nodded, unable to reply, as he had placed a bite of ice cream and cone in his mouth just as she spoke. He pointed at her, smiling, as if affirming her flirtatious response. He swallowed and responded, "Touché."

Chad was finished first. He unceremoniously stuffed

the napkin into the cup and sat back and looked over at Hope to see her progress. "Slow poke. It'll melt soon if you don't hurry up," he teased.

"I'll get it done before it melts. I'm almost finished, smartass," she chided him as she grinned, sticking the spoon in her mouth and licking it clean.

Hope sneaked a peek again as Chad grinned, shaking his head, letting his hands dance on the wheel of the truck. "Okay. My turn to ask a question. What is something you want to do before you die?" he asked and leaned his head back, awaiting her response.

Hope pondered the question, squinting one of her eyes shut as she thought. She took a bite of her ice cream, letting the thoughts fester before responding, "I would love to see Bora Bora one day. What about you?"

"Bora Bora, huh?" He looked over at her. "The French Polynesians are supposed to be pretty stellar, that's for sure." Chad looked forward over the steering wheel as he thought. "Hmmm, what would I like to do before I die?" He drummed his fingers across the rim, "I think I'd love to have a daughter one day." Chad turned his head to see her reaction. "Too sappy? Did I just lose my man card?" He arched his brow, that keen smirk appearing.

Hope's ovaries could burst at that moment, but she also laughed lightly at his hesitation. "You want a daughter?" She set her spoon down in her half-melted soft serve, her tone softened and moved by his response. "What about a son?"

Chad smiled. "Well, a son would be fantastic, but I always thought little girls and their dads always look great. I never had a sister, I don't have any nieces. I just think it'd be special to have a little girl."

Hope was speechless. "Really? A little girl? I think that

is so precious." She took the silence to finish her ice cream, offering to take his cup so they could clean up. Chad's cheeks filled with color at her remark, but waved her hand away.

"Nope, I treat today, remember?" He reached over and took her cup and napkins, jumping out of the truck to throw their cups away in the trash can a few strides away. Sliding back into his seat and buckling his seatbelt, he turned to her and said, "We have to go home, don't we?"

Hope's heart sunk slightly, but she nodded slowly. "Yes, unfortunately adulting is a responsibility that still happens on the weekend."

"Oh, that shit, adulting." He shook his head, grinning back at her as he pulled out of the parking lot.

Hope smiled back at him; in fact, she smiled the whole way home, even more so when she felt his hand reach for hers, interlacing their fingers. She looked up at him when they stopped at a light and Chad looked back, their eyes connecting. Her cheeks burned, but in that moment, that magical moment of connection, she didn't care. What she cared about was that his hand was with hers, and she squeezed appreciatively as she felt the truck move forward.

Chad skillfully moved through the neighborhood and onto her street, as if he had known where she lived for decades. He pulled into her driveway, almost painfully slowly, reluctantly letting go of her hand to park.

Chad looked over at her and smiled. "Don't move. I'm opening your door."

Hope nodded. "Okay. I'll wait."

Chad slid out of his seat and she watched as he walked around the front of the truck and opened her door, offering his hand to her, which she gladly took. The tingles she'd been feeling did not die down after holding his hand;

in fact, the electricity running through her veins was intensified.

Hope naturally slid her hand in the crook of his elbow once her feet hit the ground. She had only done it a few times tonight, but it felt so right, and he gave her hand a gentle squeeze. Chad walked Hope to her front door, and they both stood at the top of the stairs, looking at each other. She didn't want this moment to end, and his choice to remain silent signaled it was mutual.

Hope broke the silence. "Chad, thank you for lunch, ice cream, the tour of the city, and the incessant cheesy jokes. I had a really good time." She smiled shyly.

Chad looked down at her as he leaned against the door and smiled. "I feel the same way; it was a great time. We need to do that again?" he questioned, that arched brow showing up again.

Hope smiled. "Definitely. We *definitely* should do it again." Then there was that silence again. *We're getting good at the silence*, she thought. Hope took advantage of the delay, and committed everything about this moment to memory. The way Chad stood, his proximity to her own body, how he smelled, his masculine woodsy cologne now mixed with the scent of pizza, coffee, and chocolate. It was sweet, and intoxicating.

Before she could say anything more, Chad broke the proximity Hope was admiring. "See you on Monday for coffee?" Chad was already turning toward the stairs, before Hope could respond.

Hope's smile was much smaller now. "Yes. Remember, the coffee's on me." She was disappointed, her expectations not met. Wait, what was she expecting? Did she read too far into this date? Yes, clearly so. Hope unlocked her screen door and pulled it open, turning to wave goodbye.

Hope knew Chad was completely still at the top of the steps, watching her unlock the door. Before she knew what was happening, Chad moved back up next to Hope, cutting her inevitable 'bye' short. He cradled her face in his hands, and she sighed at how perfectly her face fit in his palms. They were calloused and worked, but gentle. It was only then she felt the soft velvet of his lips against her own. She closed her eyes and the surge of sensation that ran through her body lifted her on her tippy toes. She raised her hand and cupped his hand against her cheek, returning the kiss with the same sweet passion as it was offered.

He broke the kiss, but cradled her face longer, placing his forehead against hers. He offered that brilliant smile again, and Hope had to do everything she could to tame her heart, but she was grinning up at him too. She swore he could hear it thumping against her chest. Chad caressed the temples of her face for a brief second and then dropped his hands and jogged down the stairs to his truck. Hope remained at her door, watching him pull out of her driveway, neither of them waving goodbye. She didn't want that moment to have a final point. She needed to let it linger.

chapter
six

CHAD

HE WATCHED HER UNLOCK THE screen door, one hand clutching the pizza box to her hip. The last smile she flashed him left him wanting. He felt the flinch, he read her body language, and he hoped to heavens he didn't read her wrong. Chad left his doubts to his mind and made a split second, completely impulsive, decision. He bolted to her side, his hand gripping the screen door to keep it from opening.

Then he cradled her face in his hands, and gazed at her. Her eyes tore at his soul, consuming him, and she didn't even have to try. He leaned forward and pressed his lips against hers. God, she tasted sweet, just as he'd imagined. Hope intoxicated him, and he wanted more. But he stopped, knowing he had to be the one to break this moment of perfection.

He pressed his forehead to hers, unable to stop the grin. That moment, that electric - dare he say, magical - moment, lit a fire within him that he hadn't felt in a long time. She was fucking beautiful and he didn't want to leave.

His thumbs stroked her temples a moment longer, as he took her in. That grin she gave him sealed the deal, and knew the feelings were mutual.

Chad knew if he didn't get back into his truck, he would push for more, and he didn't want to ruin this. Hope was different, special, and he was going to cherish her and these moments as he should. He was not going to rob himself of this as he had done in the past. He had to bolt down the stairs and into his truck before he regretted anything he did. He prayed that Hope would be left with the same intense sensation he had felt in his chest and that his darting away wasn't a sign he didn't want more. In fact, it was quite the opposite.

When Chad arrived home, he set his keys on the mini-raised counter. Sliding his shoes off, he paused. His fingers traced his lips, still smiling. Hope wanted this. She had to, with that brilliant eye-glinting grin she gave him. He had to rein himself in and the only answer to this was a cold shower. His third shower of the day, his second shower because of Hope.

CHAD PUSHED BACK FROM HIS metal desk and looked at the clock, running his hand through his short hair. He was close to shutting the lights off in his office and heading out but he had to make sure his Major delegated the mission duties on to other members of his unit. He pulled his office door open and walked down the hall; the Major's door was ajar and he walked in. "Hey, LaCrosse. Did you manage to get those orders out to the Lieutenants?"

A tall, well-built black man looked up from his desk and nodded. "Evening, Colonel. Yes. The LTs received the orders before lunch. They should be nearly finished delegating them out. I gave them until Wednesday to have all of the work completed."

"Good. We have thirty more to do before next week." Chad leaned against the doorway during the exchange.

"Yes, and we have about 150 more logistical issues we need to address before we hit the field in two weeks. Shit is going to hit the fan if this doesn't get done." Major LaCrosse stood, picking up his empty mug. "Coffee?"

"I'm grabbing some off base once I leave, but we can walk down to the lounge." Chad continued as they walked down the hall together, "The men will need to tighten up; there's absolutely no reason why these issues weren't addressed weeks ago - wait, no - months ago. If there are deficits, they will pay in dividends out in the field." Chad walked through the empty lounge with Major.

"No shit. We need to address missing links within leadership. The men are pushing themselves, and this isn't an issue of if they're working or not. But we need to figure out where the missing link is with the orders. These orders aren't new; we're just giving them again." Major poured his coffee into a styrofoam cup and capped it.

"Oh, I know. Some don't go home until twenty four hundred and are back by zero four thirty. They will be battle-worn before hitting combat next fall." Chad's brows were furrowed as he discussed the issues within his unit. It wasn't unusual to have logistical issues with mission and field trainings, but their deployment was imminent, and these things needed to be smoothed out sooner rather than later.

Chad and Major LaCrosse finished their conversation

before heading their separate ways. Chad entered his office to grab his cover, keys, and wallet, and strode out of the building. He placed his cover on his head and walked to his car. He returned the salute of several enlisted Marines as they walked to their cars. "Have a good evening, gentlemen," he responded. He always strived for professionalism, and knew the men and women who worked under him went home to friends and families, too. They deserved to have pride in their work, and if sending them off with a friendly farewell meant their day ended on a better note, then so be it. Why would he walk all over them? He always made an effort to acknowledge good work and actions, regardless of rank.

He used the handle on the inside of his truck and pulled himself up into the seat. The light scent that lingered in his truck, or in his mind, reminded him of Hope. He smiled as he pulled the door closed; he would see her soon enough. Chad was tempted to visit her on Sunday, but didn't want to be *that* guy. He savored their kiss, and replayed it over and over. He felt insane; he never felt this way about a woman. Typically, Chad's relationships were short and hot, but sizzled quickly, usually because he had to leave for field training, or deployment. In fact, a lot of his relationships ended in betrayal. He never had an official "Dear John" letter; many of the women he had dated over the years just couldn't handle being alone for long periods of time. They needed the constant companionship. At least, that's what they told him if they ended it. If he ended them, it was usually because he couldn't handle the clinginess. He had a tendency to fall for flat girls - the girls who simply liked the idea of being on the arm of an officer, but didn't care for the responsibilities.

He sighed, running his hand over his head. This must be his nervous tick, just like when Hope tucked her hair behind her ear. Chad smiled, thinking of her. She was different from the other girls he'd known. She had so many layers he wanted to peel away and explore. He loved that she could play the guitar; he didn't know when he would tell her that he missed playing and singing. Yes, this United States Marine sang in church growing up. He shook his head. It'll come out eventually, but it was something he hadn't pursued for a long time. He would never be able to keep up with her.

What was he doing, besides stalling? He put his truck in gear and reversed out of the parking spot, heading toward the coffee shop. Chad glanced at the clock. Damn, it was late. Koffeehaus was going to close in an hour. He was lucky that it wasn't far from base; in fact, it was only two stoplights away, but he wanted to spend as much time with Hope as he could.

As he pulled into the small parking lot that surrounded the small building, he peered inside to see if she was busy. It looked empty, thankfully. Hope was wiping down the tables, and he could see her swaying, bouncing to some tune. He admired her briefly, eager to see her face to face. Chad completed his wardrobe exchange in record time and slid out of the truck to replace his boots with sneakers. Tucking his wallet into his back pocket, he locked his truck's door and walked up to the coffeehouse, eagerly opening the door to hear the bell.

Hope was bent over, picking up a napkin when he walked in, and she turned at the sound of the bell.

"Hey, Hope. It was a really long day. I couldn't get out any earlier." He walked closer to her, watching for her response.

Hope's face lit up when she saw him and that was the response Chad was looking for. "Oh, hi Chad!" She stood, throwing the trash in the bin, coming up to him, unlike any other time, but she stopped short. He saw the hesitation on her face, but that million-dollar smile remained.

He didn't hesitate, though. He reached out and wrapped his arms around her, and he felt her body form to his. She fit; every bit of her fit in his arms. Chad held her for a moment, offering a gentle squeeze before letting go, and kissed her cheek affectionately. "How was your day?"

He saw the color rise in her cheeks, and her shy smile appeared. "It was a Monday. Nothing special." She slipped her hand into his, interlacing her soft fingers with his calloused ones, and led him to the counter. He smiled at the gesture; it was a sign to Chad she was comfortable with his affection. This was a huge shift for them. They were just casual coffee friends on Friday, and physically affectionate friends - perhaps more - by Monday.

"I was beginning to worry I wouldn't make it before you closed." He smiled at her and leaned over the counter as she looped around to take his order.

"Well, *I* was beginning to wonder if I scared you off Saturday." She gave him a side glance before laughing. It was light, but he knew the statement held partial truth, even though she also was kidding.

"No, there was no scaring me off on Saturday. It would require a little more than pizza, beer, and ice cream to do that." He made a notable pause, watching her face. "And a kiss, of course." He grinned as he saw her face light up at the mention of that intimate moment they shared.

"Well, good. I had a great time with you." She slid the coffee cup she was preparing while they talked across the counter. "I didn't forget that I was treating you to coffee this week."

He took the cup appreciatively, knowing he would regret the caffeine so late, but he wouldn't refuse a cup offered by Hope. "Thanks. Want to grab a mug and we can sit together until someone comes in?"

Hope looked around the store for a moment and then nodded. "Sure. I'll make myself some tea. It won't leave me wired for the rest of the night."

"Hey, if I get wired, I'm coming over to your place to keep you up," he joked as he made his way to the condiment counter.

"I sleep like a rock. I wouldn't hear you knocking, but I can always make you some tea," she jested back, grinning at him.

"No. I'm good. You just forget I'm a Marine. I have ways." He poured the sugar into his coffee, stirring it with a small wooden stirrer.

"Yeah, you and your spidey ways, I'm sure." She smiled as he watched her pour her hot water into her mug. There was a twinkle in her eye again, and that smile made his heart skip a beat. He paused and leaned his elbow on the counter, waiting for her to come around. "Where do you want to sit?" she said as she made her way to him.

She stopped in such close proximity to him, he could lean over and press his lips to hers if he so chose, but he maintained his composure and stood up from his lean. "Comfy chairs are nice, no?"

"Always."

Chad allowed her to lead the way, and his eyes didn't fail to watch her from behind. That kiss they shared lit that fire, and he couldn't help but admire her petite hourglass form. She fit against him so perfectly, he craved to feel her that way again.

"So nothing interesting happened today?" He settled in his chair, crossing his leg over one knee. He smiled as she pulled her legs up underneath her and curled up in the chair. She was cute, and the movement was so natural, as she cocooned herself in with her mug of tea.

That smile still remained as they spoke. "Nothing really. Our big weekly shipment came in, so I did some inventory. Other than that, same ol', same ol'. What about you?"

He grunted with disapproval of the reflection of his day. "Same shit, different day." He shook his head, taking a sip of his coffee.

"So, Chad." Hope dropped her knees and sat cross-legged in the chair, leaning toward him affectionately. "Tell me what you do in your free time, outside of running." Her face was thoughtful, and rosy at the apples of her cheeks.

Chad let out a soft chuckle, leaning back in his chair, tapping a finger to his chin as he thought. "Well" - he looked at her with a mischievous glimmer in his eye - "I like coffee, and long walks on the beach." He grinned, shaking his head. "No, I don't have a lot of free time, but what I would like to do if I *did* have free time is pick up the guitar again." Chad winked at Hope.

"Wait. Did you just tell me you play guitar?" Hope set her cup down, her face dumbfounded with surprise.

Chad nodded. "It's been awhile, maybe years, since I've sat down and played. I literally have been going from deployment, to training, to promotion, to deployment, to training..." He motioned with his hand in a circular path.

Hope tilted her head to the side, a sad expression pressed to her face. "Do you have a guitar with you?"

"No, I gave my guitar away a few duty stations ago." Chad rested his mug on his bent knee, offering a smile to Hope. He was fascinated with her sadness about his guitar.

"Well that needs to be fixed," Hope declared, returning the smile.

"Probably won't happen for some time. We are deploying by end of the year, and it is only going to get crazier. I don't even know where to start looking for one here in Jax." His colloquial reference to the city made Hope smile.

"Well, that's an easy fix. I'll help." She diverted the conversation, and Chad felt it may have been to avoid any unease on his part. He really wasn't uncomfortable with the subject matter; it was simply that his job took over his life.

"We also call Jacksonville, Florida, 'Jax' too," Hope piped in.

"Makes sense; we're too lazy for three syllables," Chad replied, laughing at his own joke. "Do you miss your Jax?" He hoped he wasn't treading into rough terrain.

Hope smiled, that small, yet still bright smile. Chad awaited her reply in the pregnant pause. "Yes, yes, I miss *my* Jax," she replied. "I think I miss my Dad and sister the most." Hope paused and took a long-drawn sip of her tea. Chad loved how she stirred the tea before lifting it to her lips. "I talked to Dad and Harper, my sister, this weekend. Harper is coming around. She took my mom's death real hard, and then, when I moved away, it made things worse. Dad has her in counseling, but they may come up to visit this summer. It was good to hear his voice. Harper sounded a lot more like herself. She was excited about staying with me for a few weeks, if Dad could stand it." Hope smiled.

"You're close with your family...I can tell, just by how you're talking about them. I can see why losing your Mom would rock your world, and theirs too," Chad observed. "My family wasn't particularly close. I don't think I've talked to my parents or brother in months, maybe even a year. I don't even know if they know I moved to Camp Lejeune." Chad paused for a moment, reflecting on his own personal life. "I guess that's partly my fault too, but growing up wasn't a walk in the park either." Chad shrugged. "It's fine, though. I've got great buddies in my unit and of course, now my coffee fiend buddy here." He lifted his mug toward her in a feigned toast.

Hope smiled at his reflection. "Yes, family is and was my everything, but I needed to get away to put myself back together. This coffeeshop, Mrs. Lulu...and you, are bringing me around." Chad watched Hope's face fill with color when she mentioned him, and he couldn't help but hide a smile behind his mug. Hope added, "I do miss writing, though. That older couple I told you about before? The ones who come in just about every day for tea and a bakery item in the afternoon? I really want to write their story."

"Then do it. What's stopping you?" Chad encouraged her. "I know you said you left it behind you, but maybe this is a way for you to heal. Write your way back to healing your heart." Chad was surprised at his own romantic approach.

"I've been chewing on it all day." Hope shrugged. She looked up through the glass door of the entrance of the coffeehouse. "I purposely didn't bring my laptop with me. I brought my tablet to suffice my technology needs. Until now, I never needed anything more. I knew that I would get to this point, but it's okay; the writing urge will pass."

Hope stood up and walked to the door, locking it. Chad watched her figure in her charming apron turn around. "I hope you're okay with helping me close tonight. I might just put you to work." She grinned. Chad's heart leaped at her smile. He would do anything she asked at this point.

Chad tucked her writing urge in the back of his mind. He would somehow help her to write. He didn't know how, but he would. "Sure, maybe I'll earn myself more coffee credit," he joked as he stood, tipping the last bit of his coffee out of his mug.

"I was only kidding, and coffee will *always* be on me." She winked at him as she walked by. Her fingers slid up his left arm, dragging across his skin and the fabric of his shirt. She was flirting and Chad loved it. He stood to follow her.

At first, Hope refused to let Chad help but once Chad grabbed the broom from behind the counter and started working, she relented. At one point, Hope turned on her music, and Chad loved how drawn she was to it. He was even more entertained when he watched her sway in what he would call an attempt to dance while she organized the mugs, plates, and utensils behind the counter. He teased her relentlessly, "You really should stick to singing and the guitar," and grinned at her while mopping the floor.

"You're not the first to say that," she laughed, throwing a dirty rag at him.

Fuck. He could tackle her right there and take her, but his common sense kicked in and he remained tethered to the mop.

Every now and then, she would throw out bits of knowledge about sanitizing surfaces, how to store dirty rags, and if his mopping was sufficient. Chad didn't want her to stop singing, dancing, or talking to him; he'd spend the whole night here if she just continued.

Once Hope was satisfied with the state of the coffee-house, she lifted her apron off her shoulders, folded it, and tucked it in her shoulder bag.

"Ready to go?" Hope asked as she made her way toward the windows and lowered the blinds over the glass.

"I'm ready if you are. May I walk you to your car?" Chad replied, standing by the glass entrance door.

Hope laughed at his offer. "Sure, but my car is right there." She pointed to the small silver sedan sitting only a few parking spots away from the entrance.

Chad shrugged his shoulders. "You never know if there are rabid cats."

Hope laughed heartily, her head falling back as she covered her mouth. "Rabid cats? Where the hell did you get rabid cats from?" She turned the lights in the coffee-house off and walked toward Chad at the entrance.

Chad shrugged his shoulders again and winked at her as he unlocked the door and pushed it open. "You just never know. I'm sure I had a rabies vaccine, considering all the shots I get through the military."

"Oh good, I'm glad to know one of us is protected if we get bit by a random, rabid cat," she laughed, her hand grazing across the front of his abdomen as she walked by. He loved that she touched him while she passed near him. It made him feel alive.

Chad stepped back as Hope locked the door. When she turned to walk toward her car, he placed his hand on the small of her back, and smiled at her when she looked up. When they reached her car, Hope turned to bid him farewell. "Thank you for helping me close tonight." She placed her hand gingerly against his waist.

Chad closed the already small space between them, gazing down at her darkened face, the street lamp highlighting only the outline of her face. He lifted his hand up and let his thumb trace over her cheekbone before responding. "It was my pleasure. If I didn't have to be on base by seven, I'd try to stay longer." Chad took a moment to study her, to memorize her face. Hope had closed her eyes when he touched her face. He lifted his other hand and cupped her face in his palms and leaned in.

Chad pressed his lips against hers, teasing with his tongue, letting it slide across the entrance of her mouth. His heart skipped a beat when she pressed her small frame against his and her lips parted against his, encouraging him. He held her at the nape of her neck, deepening the kiss, their tongues dancing. He wanted to devour her with his passion, but he broke the kiss. He felt her lower against the car in resigned defeat, both bodies breathless. Chad held her close for a moment, before he heard her break the silence.

"I like when you do that," she whispered, pressing her cheek against his chest, her arms wrapped around his waist loosely.

Chad chuckled, his fingers tangled in her hair, letting the sweet moment linger. He craved feeling her like this. "What is it that you like?"

He felt her smile and Hope looked up at him. she touched her hand to her cheek. "The way you hold my face when you kiss me." The light trickling over her features gave her deep crimson cheeks away.

He leaned forward and pressed a lingering kiss on her forehead, his hands naturally cupping her face once again. "Okay, then I'll keep doing it."

He felt her laugh softly against him. "Promise?"

He had to laugh at her persistence. "I promise." His

first promise of hopefully many, he thought. Chad reached behind her and unlatched her car. "See you tomorrow?"

Hope hesitantly sat in the driver's seat, but left the door open, "I'll be here. Good night, Chad."

He nodded, closing the door and stepping back onto the sidewalk. "Good night, Hope."

chapter *seven*

HOPE

*C*HIRRRRRRP. THE FAMILIAR SOUND WOKE Hope from her deep slumber. It was Saturday morning and that tone meant Chad was awake. She stretched lazily, moving from her side to her back, and yawning. Her arms extended upward, grazing the back of her headboard, before rolling over and reaching for her phone to see what Chad was up to this early in the morning.

> **Good morning, beautiful.**

Hope smiled at his greeting. She tapped reply to enter her response.

> **Good morning, handsome. How'd you sleep?**

Hope hit the send button, letting the phone rest on her chest until she heard Chad's designated notification on her phone.

> **Not bad. Much better if you were here.**

Hope shook her head. He had a way with words.

Well, if you are up for morning breath, and bed head hair then you're welcome to join me in bed.

She grinned playfully, half-hoping he would show up.

Be there in 15.

Awesome. I can't wait, I have a surprise. Show up in PJs or you're banned from the bed.

Hope dropped her phone on the bed, excited to give him his surprise. Chad was a man of his word; he showed up when he said he would. He was never late. She darted into the bathroom to brush her teeth. As close as they had become in the past three months, since their first real date, she was still not ready to share her true morning self. After she washed her face, she brushed her blonde hair back and into a messy bun at the top of her head.

Hope quickly swapped her sleep clothing for a casual cotton tank she wore on the weekends - dark pink was her choice today - and cotton shorts. It was then she heard her notification, indicating Chad's reply.

Funny, I have something for you too. Be there a little late, I am picking up breakfast and coffee too. Don't worry, I'm in weekend clothes.

Hope laughed tapping a response before throwing the phone back on the bed.

Fair enough. You know where the key is. See you soon.

She returned her attention to picking up the loose clothing scattered in her room. The rest of her home was fine, but her room was never picked up unless Chad was coming over. Once it was acceptable, Hope headed to the kitchen. She knew he was bringing coffee but they were both coffee fiends and refills would most certainly be needed.

Standing in front of one of Chad's first random surprises - he upgraded her coffeemaker to an automated grinder and coffee maker duo - she pushed the button to delay the brew she scheduled the night before by an hour. He always came over on Saturday mornings, and she always went over to his place on Sunday, if he wasn't working. If it was possible, Hope and Chad were together. They ran errands, did laundry at each other's homes, and went gallivanting into cities outside of Jacksonville. Hope ached to be with him whenever they were apart, and by Chad's eagerness to be over early every weekend, it was affirmation that feeling was mutual.

It was only last week that Chad drove Hope to the beach, Emerald Isle, thirty-two miles southeast of Jacksonville. He remembered that it was the one-year anniversary of the accident and Hope was not up for fun shenanigans. Chad remembered how she had said she found the most peace by the sea. They spent hours sitting on the beach, Chad holding Hope through her waves of tears. It was that weekend that Hope shared the sweetest memories of her mother, and Chad listened. It was that weekend Hope knew she loved Chad.

Hope opened the panel track blinds over the glass

sliding doors facing her small fenced-in backyard. She turned when she heard a key inserted into her door. *Chad.* He was here. She made her way to the door and swung it open before he could pull the key out.

"Good morning!" She pressed a quick tender kiss on his cheek.

"Morning, dollface." Chad's eyes lit up when he saw her, which made Hope tingle inside. She reached out and took the drink carrier from him. "I taste mint, I thought I was going to experience morning breath," he teased.

"If I could ever prevent you from morning breath, I will," Hope laughed, making room for him to come in, and looked at his clothing. "Those are *not* your pajamas; those are gym shorts and a tank."

Chad walked in, now holding plastic bags with styrofoam boxes filled to the brim with food. "Well you can't talk much; you aren't really wearing your sleepwear." He swatted playfully at Hope's bottom, making his way to the back door. "Breakfast outside? We might as well take advantage of it before it gets too hot."

Hope laughed as she followed. "Sure, but where is your surprise?" she exclaimed, like an excited child.

"Patience, grasshopper, patience." He looked back at her, winking. "And you had one too, don't forget. So once *you* put up, *I* will."

"Psh, I can wait," Hope challenged as she followed Chad out the glass door. She set the bag and coffee down on her outdoor table. "I'll go get the cushions and table cloth. Do we need utensils or napkins?"

Chad searched through the bags, shaking his head. "Nope, they packed it all. But you're forgetting something." He waved her back.

"What's that?" Hope peeked into the bag to look for a clue.

Chad turned her around, and wrapped his hands around her face, pressing a short, sweet kiss against Hope's lips. She smiled, wrapping her arms around his waist. "You forgot my sugar." Chad grinned at his own play on words, nipping her lower lip before swatting her bottom again.

"I always have sugar for you," Hope cooed back at him as she stepped inside to gather the comfort items she stored inside to avoid weathering. She came out, arms overfull and stacked, and felt his arms lift some of the items from her grasp. "Thanks," she breathed, still smiling at him.

Hope watched as Chad quickly set out the cushions. It was clear he was used to this routine outside and was familiar with the process. "Let me help you with the tablecloth."

"Sure." They stretched the fabric over the wrought iron table and divvied out the boxes, setting each other's places. "So, what's for breakfast today?"

"Cheese and bacon scramble, hash browns, and French toast with real maple syrup." Chad lifted the warmed bottles of pure maple syrup. Hope knew instantly Chad went to Nottingham's, their favorite breakfast place. It was a locally-owned place that jam-packed their boxes with food when they ordered to-go.

"Ooooh. My favorite!" Hope exclaimed as she settled into her chair.

"I know." Chad patted her hand fondly as he popped open the boxes. Just like their first date, Chad insisted on serving Hope when he brought the food. Hope found it endearing and enjoyed serving him when it was her turn.

They both ate quietly, exchanging few words here and there, simply enjoying each other's presence. Just like their first ice cream, the silence didn't scare them. They found comfort just knowing the other was there. Chad always finished first, and Hope found it humorous, especially when he claimed it was his officer training.

He leaned back against the chair, resting his head in his hands. "It really is a nice day," he mused while Hope took her last few bites.

She nodded, cutting her last bite of French toast in half. "Best morning in a while. I'm glad it's the weekend."

Chad stood from his chair, grinning. "Me too. Stay here, I'm running to the truck real quick. I'll be right back."

Hope waved at him as she leaned over her box to take her last bite, nodding. She knew he was going to retrieve whatever surprise he had for her. She was going to wait to give him hers. They never had surprises for each other at the same time, but they enjoyed finding things for each other that they knew meant a lot to the other. She finished her meal and gathered the trash together.

Chad walked back in, holding a wide white box in his arms. He held it against his chest as he made his way back to the table, a mild distressed look on his face, which Hope noticed immediately.

"What's wrong, Chad? Did something happen to it?"

Chad shook his head. "No. I have the purest intent not to upset you with this. I just want you to know I got this for you because I believe in you, and I want you to pursue what you were meant to do." He gingerly placed the box on her lap, only stepping back when Hope secured it against herself.

Hope gave him a hesitant look, unsure what he was implying, until she saw the imprinting on the box. A gray Apple. Chad had purchased her a MacBook Pro. The emblem stared right at her. Hope was speechless. The gift was incredibly generous, and she knew instantly why he had given it to her. Her eyes began to fill with tears, she set the box on the table and stood.

Chad quickly added, "I really didn't mean to upse- " Hope broke his sentence, wrapping her arms around his neck and pressing a fierce kiss against him.

"No," she said. This time, her hands cupped his face as she stood on her tippy toes. "You are the kindest, most thoughtful soul I have ever met." Tears streamed down her cheeks. She was overwhelmed with emotion. "You have never read anything I've written, but yet, you believe in me."

Chad smiled, wiping away the tears that wet her face. "Why wouldn't I? I see it when you talk to me about your ideas. I see it when you write me notes, and cards. You were meant to write. So write. I don't care what you did before, but you need to write now." Hope's heart nearly burst with joy. She leaned her head on his shoulder, keeping him in a tight hug. He wrapped his muscular arms around her, holding her to himself. "So, you're not upset?"

Hope stepped back, patting his chest affectionately. "No. Definitely not upset. You wouldn't guess that I was looking at laptops on my tablet the last few weeks."

Chad smiled. "No, I didn't. I'm glad I gave this to you now then. I beat you to gifting this to yourself."

Hope laughed, pressing another affectionate kiss on his cheek. "I can't wait to open this. I've never had a Mac. I've always, always, *always* wanted one."

"I'm guilty, I googled what laptop is good for an author and Apple seemed to win the contest. I'm not sure why, but here it is. We can always exchange it." Chad ran his hand over the box.

"No, this is more than I could ever get myself. This is really generous. I can design my own covers and teasers with the software that comes with Mac," she added, tracing the Apple emblem with her fingers. She dropped her hand and looked up at him, her eyes filled with realization. "Wait here, it's my turn."

Hope ran inside the house, pushing the glass door closed behind her. Her gift wasn't as generous when it came to how much she spent, but she was excited nonetheless. She smiled as she lifted the worn case from against the wall of her guest room and made her way out.

She paused before stepping out back to Chad, who had taken his seat. "Okay. I know this isn't new, but it is absolutely repairable. And when I saw it, it sang your name, and I had to get it. I promise to help restore it and tune it." Hope stepped out onto the porch, bringing the worn leather case out with her.

When the guitar case came into view, Chad instantly rose to greet Hope. "You got me a guitar?" Chad's voice was quiet as he took the case from her. "You bought me a guitar?" Chad's face was etched with disbelief when he asked again. "I didn't even know you could get one here in Jax. Or did you have to leave town to go get it?"

Hope smiled at his surprise. She walked behind him as she moved her laptop box off the table so he could lay the case down. "I saw it at the music store next to Nellie's a few weeks ago. They have used instruments that come and go, and I loved this one. The wood was pristine and the sound was amazing. We can always get you a new case, and I tuned it the best I could." Chad opened the case, his hand running over the smooth surface of the instrument. Hope bounced where she stood in excitement, her hands clasped together in front of her face in anticipation of his response. "So, do you like it?"

Chad shut the case and secured it. He paused before wrapping his arms around Hope's shoulders. She instantly melted against him, placing her arms around his neck again. Chad didn't have tears in his eyes, but his voice was choked. "It was thoughtful, and I adore the case." He pressed a tender kiss on her forehead, holding her close. "I never expected to own a guitar again, let alone one this beautiful."

"Oh, I am *so* excited you love it." Hope released him from the hug. "Now we can play together!"

Chad laughed as he looked at the case fondly. "It's going to take some practice to get up to par with your playing. You're far ahead of me."

Hope smiled as she picked up her box and held it against her chest. "Can we go in so we can turn this on? I can't wait to play with it. Will you help me set it up?"

Chad chuckled, nodding. "Absolutely, and I'll get to play with my guitar." He lifted the guitar case up and followed her back inside. "Trash?" he asked as they walked in.

"We can get all that later, let's play in here first!" Hope squealed as she slid the box on the coffee table and begin unpacking. Chad followed, Hope could feel his amusement as he sat behind her on the couch, running his hands over her shoulders, his fingers tangling in her hair.

Hope felt him lean forward to press a kiss on her head. "Don't worry about the trash, I'll take care of it. Let's get you writing." She smiled at his response, leaning back against his legs as she opened the box. Hope couldn't erase the grin that had been glued to her face since touching the Apple emblem.

Hope and Chad took turns playing their gifts throughout the afternoon. Chad helped Hope set up her laptop, and even went as far as making sure it was protected with a customized case. The case was dark pink, padded, with Hope's initials H.S. emblemed on the surface. Hope loved it. The urge to write never disappeared for her, and had only grown since her relationship with Chad began. The story of the Paisleys brewed in her mind and at times kept her up at night. She felt unsettled, knowing she had to write it. Chad read her, and he filled the missing piece she needed.

Chad began to strum the strings of his guitar. Hope admired the childlike amusement that spread across his face as he found his place with his guitar. It was clear he had played before, and missed the playing, in the way he hugged the instrument. He had watched Hope play, encouraged her to learn and write new songs. Chad even occasionally added his own voice, but he was in a different zone when playing the guitar, and Hope cherished that look.

Hope reached over and placed his hands and fingers on different positions and different chords. "Do you remember that song I wrote earlier?" She stroked his arm tenderly.

"Yes. The one about the raven. The one I like." He smiled at her. That smile made her burn inside, in the most wonderful way.

"I want to teach it to you. So we can play it together." Hope grinned up at him. "It was meant to be a duet." She continued the lesson and even retrieved her own guitar. It didn't take long for Chad to catch on to the chords and rhythm of the song. Chad and Hope shared their love in music, and now they shared a song.

Before Hope knew it, the sun was setting, the trash still sitting in bags outside.

After their jam session, Chad lounged on the couch watching her type her story, playing with her hair intermittently. A short while later, she turned the laptop off, and kneeled in front of Chad. She laid the top portion of her body over his, bracing against the couch. "Thank you for your gift. It's more generous than you know."

Chad stroked her upper back, tracing his fingers across her shirt. and he pressed a kiss to her temple. "Thank *you* for your gift. It was more thoughtful than you know." Hope smiled, enjoying the weight of his arms around her. Chad made her feel safe. He never judged her when she was having a bad day; he would hold her, and that's all he needed to do. He was adventurous, and kind, and loving. He was perfect, and Hope gave up on holding herself back from falling for him. He guarded her heart when she was the most vulnerable. Hope had fallen head over heels for this man, and there was nothing anyone could do about it.

chapter eight

CHAD

*C*HAD SAT IN HIS TRUCK, pressing his hands to his face. He was exhausted. His unit was going to be entering field training the following week and as a result, Chad was spending long days and nights on base. After stretching and pulling his cover off, and placing it on his front seat, he lifted his phone to text Hope.

On my way home. Can't wait to see you, baby.

He had never met someone with such intense patience before. Typically, this was where the girls usually lost their minds. Long hours, long days, and the future of being separated for weeks was not the best relationship building material. Hope was different. She knew he wasn't avoiding her, and she made sure there was a hot meal when he came home, no matter the time. He sometimes found her asleep on his couch after a long day at Koffeehaus. She was always there. Before he put his truck in reverse, he heard his phone's chime go off.

Great. I'll get dinner ready. Do you need or want anything?

No. No, he only needed her. It was their last night together before he reported back to base for six weeks of field training. He wouldn't be able to contact Hope; he was pretty sure he would be away from communication. If he could, he'd call her, but he couldn't promise her that.

He responded quickly before pulling out of his parking spot and heading off base toward home.

Just you, babe. Only need you.

He chuckled to himself; he had hit a new level of sappiness with Hope, but he didn't care. He wanted her to know how much he cared for her. The last six months were the best six months he'd had in years. Chad looked forward to every day with Hope. The only thing he hadn't experienced was waking up with her next to him. They had fallen asleep on the couch many times, but never overnight. He hadn't ever been in a relationship that didn't jump straight to sex before. Their intimacy grew every time they were together, and he cherished every second of feeling her against him. He hungered for more, but he'd never pushed her.

As he drove, he was lost in his thoughts. His hands on her body, cupping her ass. His hands explored her frame, clothed, under clothing, but never skin to skin and he craved her that way. The amount of self-control it took to keep himself chaste was immeasurable, but he cared for Hope. It was clear Hope didn't share the same level of experience he did, and he wanted that time to be special. It would be, if he had anything to do with it.

As he pulled into his driveway, Chad smiled. He loved seeing his front room light on, and Hope's car in his spot. He grabbed his rucksack to wash some laundry for training, and headed into the house.

He pushed the front door open and was greeted by an amazing seared onion and herb aroma wafting in his home, and loud blaring music he didn't recognize.

"Holy shit, that smells incredible," Chad remarked. He kicked off his boots and walked into the kitchen, where he found Hope bouncing and strutting to the rhythm of the music. He snuck in and caught her at the corner of the counter from behind, wrapping his arms around her waist fondly. "Hello, beautiful. Whatever you're making smells amazing."

He felt Hope lean back into his embrace, reaching an arm backward around his neck, hugging him tight. "Hi, babe. Thank you. I thought having a special dinner before you have to go to training would be nice." She leaned far back enough to kiss him. God, her kisses made him feel the same way as that first kiss did. He never got tired of them.

"Do I have time to throw a load of laundry in and jump in the shower, or should I hold off?" His hands slid down the front of her hips, hugging her to himself. Their affection was very physical, their intense chemistry was obvious to anyone that saw them.

Hope peeked at the stove and nodded. "Go ahead. I'll finish the steaks when I hear you get out of the shower." She turned around to face him, running her hands up his waist.

Chad leaned over her, holding himself up from the counter and Hope's hands pressed against his chest as they kissed. Their lips sealed, and Hope teased Chad with her tongue dipping in to greet his. Chad groaned as he broke the kiss.

"I'm saving this for later." He smiled against her kiss before he stood up.

Hope winked. "Leave your bathroom door open, I've got an idea." With that, she turned to quickly stir whatever she was cooking on the stove so it wouldn't burn, before looking back at him.

"Oh? Really?" Chad waggled his eyebrows teasingly.

Hope batted at him playfully. "Not like that. Just go shower, I'll throw your uniforms in the wash. Just make sure they're all together."

Chad grinned at her, feigning a sulk as he made his way to his room to gather his uniforms. After placing them in a small pile in front of the washer, he showered quickly. He wasn't going to delay dinner any longer, but he needed to feel the hot water on his face to rinse off the day's stress. It reset his body. He smiled when he stepped out of the shower and reached for his towel, pressing the warm material against his body. Fuck, that was nice. She must have run them through the dryer before placing them in the bathroom. He was certainly not going to be experiencing this in training. He was re-energized and looked forward to filling his rumbling stomach.

By the time Chad walked back into the kitchen, Hope was serving their steaks on plates, topping each one with her seared onion mixture. He watched her concentration, mesmerized by her beauty. Chad could spend the night watching her do her thing, but his stomach told him otherwise. He leaned in to kiss her on the cheek. "Thank you for starting my laundry."

Hope smiled at his affection. "No problem. I got a six-pack of Black Dog on the way home today; they should be chilled by now. Grab me one, too? I'll meet you at the table."

Chad squeezed her before letting her go. "You're a woman after my own heart." He pulled open the fridge, grabbed two bottles of beer, and made his way to the table.

Hope walked in a few minutes later with two plates, choosing to sit next to him at the table. Chad rubbed his hands together, and Hope eagerly waited for his reaction. He cut into his steak. Hope nailed the readiness, perfect medium. She liked her steak the same way. He moaned in pleasure as it melted in his mouth. This was fucking good.

Hope laughed, satisfied, and started eating. They ate quietly, making casual conversation. Every so often, he ran a hand down her leg under the table appreciatively, and when they were finished, he picked up her empty plate. "Hey...I'm cleaning up, not you!" Hope protested.

"Relax. I'm just clearing the table. Meet me on the couch," Chad responded. He heard Hope grunt in disapproval and he smirked.

After he set the plates in the sink to soak, Chad made his way into his mini laundry room, where he found Hope pulling his uniforms from the washer and throwing them in the dryer. Hope looked up at him innocently.

"I was just getting this started while you cleaned up the table."

Chad gently pulled her to himself, then backed her up against the wall, growling playfully in her ear, "I wanted you on the couch." He pressed his lips against her neck, letting his tongue drag across her soft skin.

Hope let out a soft sigh before running her hands into his short hair. "I'm almost done. Meet you there?"

Chad lifted his head, and kissed his way up her neck,

her ear, and ended his affection on her lips. He broke the kiss to respond, "Fine."

Hope teased him further, sliding her hands down to his ass, squeezing with each hand, toward her own hip.

Chad grunted, nipping her lower lip. "I get to pick the movie because of that."

Hope responded, clearly pleased with herself, "That's fine, it's your night anyway."

Chad returned to the family room. When he purchased his furniture, he aimed to have couches comfortable enough to lounge on. He was glad he did because he loved his couch when Hope was here. It fit both of them comfortably when snuggled together. What caught his eye was a dark pink zippered duffel bag sitting on the loveseat. He poked it as he tossed himself on the couch, lounging languidly on the cushions. Hmm. What did she bring with her? She lived around the corner. Did she plan to stay the night?

He flipped the TV on and searched his DVR list to find the movie he wanted to watch tonight. Hope sauntered into the room and climbed onto the couch, pressing herself flush against him, her head on his chest. He wrapped his arm around her, letting it linger on her low back. She felt so good with clothes on, he couldn't imagine what it would feel like once their skin touched. Once he settled on his movie choice, he set the remote down and adjusted so she could rest on her side, him behind her, spooning perfectly, hip to hip.

Hope slipped to his side, where he replaced his hand on her waist, and she comfortably rested her head on his arm and shoulder. Her scent was intoxicating. It was a mix of her shampoo, deodorant, and just Hope - light, sweet, floral. He buried his face in her hair tenderly and pressed his lips to the back of her head. His attention was not on the movie, and clearly Hope's wasn't either.

Chad ran his fingertips over her waist, his hand resting precariously near Hope's breasts, and he felt the molding of the bra she wore. He cursed the fashion gods right now. He enjoyed when she went without a bra; he could feel the soft yet firm flesh in his palm even through her clothing. His lips traveled from the back of her head to her neck.

She smiled, and he felt the goosebumps rise under his palm when he ran them down her arm.

"What's with the duffle bag? You never bring anything over," he whispered, nipping at the back of her ear.

Hope shivered against him, a soft moan escaping at his teasing. Her response was wispy. "I wanted to stay the night. You were going to be gone, and I thought it would be nice to maximize our time together, you know?" She turned around, still on her side, just now face to face.

He pressed his lips roughly against hers, sucking the air out of her lungs, and pulled himself up and over her body. Breaking the kiss, he replied, "I get to have you all night?" His voice was hungry.

Hope laughed against him as she readily moved to be well-positioned beneath him, her thighs spread around his hips, allowing him to fit perfectly against her.

"Yes, I thought I would make sure your trash and dishes were done when you left. I'd lock your place up." Her practicality was turning him on even more.

Chad laughed at his own reaction. "Fuck, Hope. If you become more practical, I may just need to carry you over my shoulder to my bed and take you all night long." He pressed his lips to hers, still laughing. His body was rubbing up against hers, his shirt crumpling with his movement. His gym shorts hardly disguised his arousal.

Hope spoke nearly inaudibly, but very clearly. "I wouldn't protest that." She smiled when Chad paused at her response.

"You want more?" Chad hovered over her, placing random kisses over her eyes and cheeks.

"I've been wanting more, but I didn't know… how to ask or, you know, start." Hope's cheeks filled with her notorious red color.

He pressed a hungry kiss against her lips as a response, his hips now grinding against hers with no hesitation. There was no hiding his arousal any longer, and she moaned at the pressure. Her hands naturally slid under his gym shorts, her hands on his bare ass, which only encouraged him to grind against her further. He momentarily paused the kiss and moved to stand over her.

"Since you said you wouldn't protest." He grinned and leaned over her, breathless, and lifted her small frame up and off the couch. He lovingly tossed her over his shoulder, smacking her ass through her soft leggings.

He grinned at her laughter as she smacked his butt in minor retribution. He bounced her gingerly, walking into his room, and laying her on the bed. She was splayed on her back, her arms out to the side and her knees playfully bent and tucked closed. He placed his hands on the inside of her knees and pushed them open as he climbed up over her. He joked with her as he kissed her neck again, nibbling and suckling, worshipping the skin that was already exposed. "I should've gone to field training sooner."

Hope chided, as she playfully smacked his shoulder, "It had nothing to do with you leaving… maybe." Hope's laughter continued as he teased her, his tongue dragging across the top of her collar bones, exposed by the tank top.

"Sure," he grunted as he pulled her tank up from her stomach, helping her unthread each arm and over her head, tossing it off the bed. They were positioned perpendicular to the head of the bed but it didn't matter. He was going to have her, and he didn't care if he was faced the right way or not. It didn't appear Hope cared either.

"No fair, your shirt needs to come off, too." Her hands pulled at his hem, exposing his tense abs, and flexing chest as he balanced himself above her. He pulled his white shirt over his head and tossed it on the floor. He felt her sigh as he rested his skin against hers. This was their first time meeting this intimately.

He continued his exploration in silence, only responding to her soft coos and moans as he kissed along the top of her breasts. His hands slid behind her, and she lifted her upper back up, unhooking her bra, letting the ends loose next to the sides of her body. He was teasing himself as he suckled the soft flesh that formed each mound before pulling the straps down her arms, exposing the pink areola circling her nipples. He moaned at the sight of her pinkened skin, her skin already prickled with goose-bumps from all the teasing. Chad removed the fabric to expose both breasts fully to his view, and to his mouth.

It was as if Hope knew what he craved and she arched her back, offering her supple flesh to his devouring. His hand cupped one breast while his lips suckled and tasted the other. He traded from one to the next, until her nipples were aroused, like small pebbles under her skin. Hope's moans filled with aching, her fingers digging into his scalp a sign to him she wanted more.

Hope's soft moans grew louder when he hit the right spot, and rhythm. There were no words expressed except for the occasional, "Please," "More," and "*Yes*." Chad kissed down the center of her stomach, working his way south. He suckled the flesh below her belly button, his hands tugging at her cotton shorts. He hooked his fingers under the waistband, sparing her panties. With one firm tug, he cleared those slender hips and dropped them down mid-thigh, exposing her dark blue bikini cut panties. They were lined with a thin strip of lace. He groaned. Dark blue. She had this planned. She remembered his favorite color.

Hope naturally let her legs spread as Chad tended to her inner thighs. He suckled and licked his way down, stopping short of her fabric-covered nether region. He repeated the same attention to the other side. He nipped at the furthest, tender spot of her inner thigh before his fingers slipped underneath the fabric.

Her feminine scent overwhelmed him. Hope lifted her hips so he could free her body of her panties. Her womanhood exposed to him, she was fully vulnerable and open to him. Chad pressed a sweet kiss against her knee before he rose to look at her face. He stood over her once more, simply gazing at the beauty before him. He wanted to kiss her, feel her passion against him once before he focused on pleasing her.

Chad pulled her closer to him, keeping her hips on the edge of the bed. He leaned over her and sealed his lips to hers. He felt her tease back, their tongues meeting, and dancing. She was breathless, her hands grabbing at his waist, pulling him down against herself. He growled into the kiss.

"I want to taste you," he moaned as he broke the kiss.

Hope smiled, stroking his cheek affectionately as he slid back down between her thighs. He wrapped his arms around the outside of her thighs as he teased his lips over her inner flesh, with small circles, suckles, and tender nibbles, making his way to the sensitive center. When Chad reached her labia lips with his tongue, he pulled her closer against his mouth. One of his hands held her tender, soft lips open, exposing her clitoris. He rolled the tip of his tongue over the soft mound. He smiled when he heard her moan, and felt her hips rise, trying to alleviate the pressure he was building in her with his teasing. He braced his other hand on her lower abdomen, making her feel every lap he took of her.

He slid his tongue further south and dipped within her. Once he tasted her, he wanted more, and the more she writhed, the more her soft moans escaped her lips, the more eager he was to take her further. Chad continued to brace her, and found his satisfaction when he heard the sudden surge of pleasure run through her, her small form tremoring beneath his grip. He savored the orgasm, doing his best to extend it, letting one thumb roll over her clit with each dip of his tongue, internally and externally stimulating her at the height of her peak.

He only relented when he felt her writhing subside, and he rose from his kneeling stance, kissing up her body. Chad wrapped his arms around her tenderly and dragged her up the bed, angling her head on his pillow. He climbed up and over her, mesmerized by the heavenly pleasured look on her face. He pressed a kiss against her ear.

"I have you all night, right?"

chapter *nine*

HOPE

*C*HAD INTOXICATED HOPE WITH HIS kisses, and she wrapped her arms around his neck and shoulders when he towered over her. She was still recovering from her first orgasm when she heard him ask her, "I have you all night, right?" His voice was gruff, and it was clear to her he was hungry. She felt the same but she was swimming in her own world of pleasure at the moment.

Her hands traveled down his back as he kissed her ear, neck, and chest once more. She needed to take his shorts off. She wanted to feel all of him against her. Any surface area of skin that touched his blazed with desire. Her hands headed southward and Chad took her hint. He pulled off his pants, and flung them to the side of the bed. They were both naked, full skin to skin touching, and Hope was completely content.

Chad lowered himself against Hope, his full arousal made obvious to her. He added pressure, catching his engorged penis between them. Hope paused him for a moment, hoping she wouldn't break this passionate moment.

"Do you have… a…?" Hope stroked his engrossed face with affection.

Chad chuckled at her hesitancy and leaned over to press a kiss to her forehead as he stretched out to reach in his nightstand. "Yes, I have a condom, babe."

Hope was relieved at his laughter and action. She pressed soft tender kisses across his shoulder and arm as he tore the small package and armed himself with the condom. He resumed pressing kisses on her breasts. She cupped his face in her hands as he suckled on each of her nipples again.

Her body ached to feel him. To feel him between her thighs, to feel him inside of her. She whimpered softly, and Chad took the cue, moving between her hips. She felt him line himself up with her, leaning his head over hers. Hope's arms wrapped around his neck as her thighs spread open, feeling him there.

Chad pressed his lips to hers, his most passionate kiss with her yet, his arms around her body, cradling her. Hope swam in the passion, her body responding, her hips rising as she felt him take over her senses. Then he slid inside her, his girth surprising her in the most pleasurable way possible.

That connection was all that Hope needed. She was lost in Chad's world. He was a fierce lover, and each thrust pushed Hope to a new brink, a new level of ecstasy. Her moans were only interrupted when he kissed her, their bodies thrusting and entwining with each other.

She trembled as she approached her second peak and, for a brief moment, she was concerned it was much too soon, but she heard Chad's moans turn into a low growl with each thrust. Breathless, he held her, cradled her in his arms, his groans raspy and low, as she moved her fingers into his scalp. His hips pressed into her rapidly, more desperately, signaling his nearing climax, as she rose to meet each of his thrusts, signaling her similar state. No words were needed, and she succumbed to the passion.

Chad pressed his forehead to hers, and pinned her hands above her shoulders. Hope was trapped beneath him, and all she could think about was how intimately amazing he felt within her. Her own body swung upward, sinking her mind into a whirlwind of pleasure. She felt his release inside her, and met his body at his peak. His thrusts grew slow and short, as he milked himself inside her, her body riding the moment with him.

Chad rested his weight over her, closing the space between their bodies. Hope wrapped her arms around him, a thin sheen of sweat coating both of them, her hands stroking his skin. After a few moments, Chad shifted to lay beside her. Hope felt Chad wrap his arm around her, pressing a tender kiss to her ear. There were no words they had to share.

Soon, Chad's breaths evened, signaling his slumber. Hope gently eased off the bed to clean up. After tending to herself, she lifted his white shirt off the floor and pulled it over her head. She crept quietly into the laundry room, her bared skin prickling to the cool air. Hope heard the soft snores as Chad slept. She pulled his uniforms out from the dryer, folding them gingerly and stacking them on the counter next to the stacked washer/dryer. She would wake up in the morning to help him pack, but she had to gather her thoughts after this passionate night.

There was nothing more delicious than feeling her Chad against her. It was far more intense than she imagined. She'd had lovers before, but never with this kind of ferocity and passion shared between them. Hope couldn't help but smile as she finished folding. Hope tiptoed her way back to the bedroom, shutting off the lights on her way. She pulled the shirt off and slid back into bed.

Chad reached out to wrap an arm around her naked waist, murmuring soft protests at her delay back to the bed. Hope turned to face him, and pressed a sweet kiss to his lips, asking softly, "What time do you have to get up?"

Chad, in his sleepy state, replied, holding her body close to his, "My alarm is set to four a.m.; you sleep in."

Saving the energy and protest for the morning, she simply nodded. A waft of sadness took over Hope. She just became the most vulnerable person to one of the most incredible men she'd ever met, and now he was going be ripped away from her for six weeks with little to no contact. The hesitancy escaped her with a heavy sigh.

Chad must've sensed her sadness and pulled her closer. She loved how he snuggled his head against hers, as if he buried his face in her hair. It was then she was one-hundred-percent comfortable, and sleep took over shortly after.

HOPE AND CHAD ONLY STIRRED after the blaring sound of the alarm woke them. Chad woke up first, shutting the alarm off. Hope felt him shift in the bed. He pulled her small body halfway underneath him, while he laid his head on her breast.

"I'm going to shave and shower, you sleep in." He spoke as if he was going to act, but his body remained completely still, and wrapping hers.

Hope laughed at the suggestion - no, the demand - as she ran her fingertips over the bare skin of the back of his arm.

"I'm awake. Remember? Morning person." She yawned, curling her naked body against his like a ball.

Chad shook his head, pressing one last kiss to the back of her neck. "You're the only morning person I like, then." He squeezed her as he left the bed. "Sleep."

Hope admired him as he walked across the room, gathering his clothing in his closet and dresser. He wasn't shy. His masculine, muscular body was Hope's Adonis fantasy. She bit her lower lip as he made his way to the bathroom, openly staring.

Hope listened to him shuffling around in the bathroom. Once she heard him turn the shower on, she snuck out of the bed. Hope pushed the door open; the steam was just beginning to drift over the top of the glassed-in shower. Chad pulled the door open with a curious look on his face and Hope grinned at him mischievously.

"I thought I would offer some help." She approached the shower, her naked form on display for him. "Maybe a quickie, perhaps?" She teased him, waving the foil-covered condom in the air. After last night, she was left wanting more of him, and hoped he felt the same way.

"Fuck, woman, you're going to be the end of me." Chad pushed the shower door open and she smiled. Hope wrapped a hand around his muscular waist, bracing against him as she stepped in. "It *does* have to be a quickie, but I'll take you whenever, and however, woman," he growled in her now dampening hair.

Hope smiled at his aggressiveness. His eagerness met her neediness for him. She felt the hot water against her skin in bursts as he shifted, letting the shower hit her. His hungry eyes were taking her naked, wet body in, and he pressed Hope against the cool porcelain wall; a contrast to the water that was beating against them.

Chad's kisses were hungry and deep. He held her face with one hand as he took her mouth with the same passion his body was moving toward. Hope lifted her leg up to the ledge of the shower, opening her hip and pelvis to him. Chad shook his head, kissing her shoulder.

"Turn around. I want you to feel every bit of me inside of you."

Hope moaned at the suggestion, dragging her nails down the front of his abdomen while she turned around, seeing Chad's eyes darken with desire. There was no hesitation. Hope felt Chad between her thighs almost instantly. He cradled one arm around her hip, bracing her hips against him. The other hand slid up her back, gripping her shoulder. In one full thrust, Chad was inside of her again.

Hope ached to feel that full thrust again and again, and Chad did not fail to deliver. The thrusts were deep, and fast. The room was filled with the sound of wet skin on skin, and all Hope could respond with were broken moans and cries of pleasure. His length dragged across the most sensitive spot within her, over and over, until she could barely hold it together.

Chad read her body language, and pulled her up in a near-standing position, changing the angle of his thrusts. He leaned over her, grunting with each thrust, "I can't wait to take you over and over again when I come back." He pulled her damp hair into a ponytail, tugging gently.

His words were the magic she needed to send her in a knee-buckling orgasm. When Chad felt her tighten and spasm beneath him, he grunted, "Fuck…" and she felt his release once again inside her, the heat rising between her thighs. His strokes slowed in rhythm, but not in depth or passion. He cradled Hope tenderly, holding her damp body against his own, and she craved that closeness he gave her.

When Chad slid out of her, she turned around to help him clean off. He leaned down to kiss her lips sweetly, still breathless from their quickie.

"You're amazing."

Hope grinned up at him through the kiss. "Thank you. You aren't so bad yourself," she teased as she reached for his washcloth and soap so she could help him wash.

Chad laughed at her response, pecking her nose with a kiss. She ran the washcloth over his chest, shoulders, and back. It was then she studied his body closer. The lines of his muscles moving with his laughter. Her fingertips traced over the wet skin, taking his body in. Hope didn't know why, but she wanted to know every inch of his body, like she knew her own.

When they were all cleaned up, Chad wrapped Hope in a towel, and then placed one around his waist. She patted his back affectionately. "You better hurry up. I'll get dressed and help you pack."

Chad and Hope worked seamlessly. Hope got dressed in fresh clothing, pulling her wet hair up in a bun, then got to work searching out the items Chad called out that he needed. Hope formed piles on the couch and dragged his rucksack into the family room for him to pack the way he needed it to be packed.

Chad, dressed in his utilities, came out, adjusting his folded sleeves above his elbow. Chad educated Hope on the width the fold needed to be and where it needed to stop and she diligently fixed the pre-folded sleeves to the desired tightness, width, and height. Chad patted Hope's arm gratefully, as he moved toward the couch.

"Wow, you rock, Hope. I couldn't have gotten this together like this without you."

"Sure you could've. You have for sixteen years, no?" she teased, as she made her way to the kitchen to make him coffee and breakfast to go.

Hope hummed her way around the kitchen, waiting for the coffee to finish brewing. She poured the hot beverage in an insulated travel mug, fixing it just the way he liked it. She stirred it with a spoon and snapped the lid on. Hope packed a small ziplock with pre-peeled hard-boiled eggs she'd grabbed from Koffeehaus the day before, and a banana already on his counter.

She glanced at the clock, growing mildly nervous at how late it was. He had to be on base at 7AM, and it was already 6:30. Before she could say anything, Hope heard the front door open, and Chad was packing the truck with his things. She should've known. Chad was never late.

Chad walked back in, and checked around the house one more time before looking at her, smiling. "You'll lock up?"

Hope returned the smile warmly. "I'll clean up, take the trash out, and lock up, yes." She offered him the ziplock, banana, and travel mug as they walked out to the truck.

Chad gratefully took the items, placing them in the truck centerfold. Chad turned to Hope, took a deep breath, and wrapped his arms around her shoulders, pressing her hard against his body. "Babe, this is the worst part."

"I know. Don't worry about me. You be safe. Call if and when you can. I'll be here when you come back,"

Hope assured Chad, squeezing him in a tight hug. She was in denial how much she would miss him.

Hope looked up at Chad, whose face was creased with wrinkles of concern. He cradled her face in his hands, his signature move, and her favorite way he started their kisses. Hope pressed her body against his as he leaned down. His soft lips touched hers, making her knees weak. He tasted like her ecstasy and made her feel complete. She wished the kiss could last for eternity.

Chad broke the kiss, and Hope stepped back, squeezing his hand one more time. She did her best to smile at him as he climbed into his truck and pulled out of the driveway. She waved at him, and watched him drive down the street, until he turned out of her line of sight. She took a deep breath before turning to return inside. The next six weeks were going to be unbearable.

chapter ten

CHAD

SIX WEEKS. SIX WEEKS WAS THE longest time Chad was apart from Hope. He'd experienced long weekends away, but he was always greeted with her presence within a few days. He threw his rucksack into the back of his cab. He ached to see her face, and to feel her hug, and more importantly, wanted her kisses and skin against him. Chad wouldn't be able to actually see Hope for another several hours. He needed to process the training before he left base. Chad begrudgingly made his way back into the building. He reciprocated multiple salutes as his enlisted and NCOs began to file out of the buildings and toward their cars. They'd get to leave base and return to their homes and families before he would. It was the price he paid for taking on the leadership role.

He walked down the empty halls, his footfalls echoing in the hallway. Chad was only encouraged that he had 72 hours of leave after he got home late tonight to be with Hope. He was pretty sure Hope was going to have to work on Friday, but he wouldn't mind staying in Koffeehaus with her while she worked. He just wanted to be with her.

Chad pushed the door open to his office and settled into his chair. Taking a deep breath, Chad lifted the first file, sorting the outcomes of the first round of field training. His Majors and Lieutenants created files for him to review on the results. He had to combine their suggestions to a final training statement for the unit and XO. After several hours, he finally pressed save on his document and attached it to the appropriate emails of those who needed it.

After sending the required email, Chad pushed away from his desk. He grabbed his cover off the hook near the door, and shut the door behind him, locking it. As he made his way back down the hall, he checked his clock and sighed. It was after midnight. There was no way Hope was still awake.

He jumped into his car with enthusiasm, thrilled he wouldn't see the base for another three days. Chad needed a shower, a hot meal, and his Hope. His pulled off his cover; he didn't want to mess with saluting with the guards at the gate, a United States Marine Corps protocol. He did offer a friendly wave as he drove off base, though.

Chad didn't go home, heading straight to Hope's house. He pulled into her driveway, and reached in his backseat to grab some clothes to drag in with him. He couldn't stand spending a night without her if he didn't have to. He pulled his phone out before getting out of the car, and texted her to see if she was awake.

Hey Beautiful. Are you awake?

It wasn't even thirty seconds before he heard the trill of his phone.

"I am now. Where are you?"

He smiled. She always left her phone on for him. She had told him she usually muted her phone, but she didn't for him.

"Outside your door."

It wasn't more than ten seconds before Hope threw open the front and screen doors, launching herself at Chad, wrapping her arms around his neck. "I missed you so much, Chad! Oh, thank you for coming to me right when you got off."

Chad chuckled at her eager greeting and held her close. "Hi, baby. I missed you more, but I smell really bad. Let me shower and we can catch up." He set her down, stroking her face fondly.

Hope led him inside and took his clothes to her room. "I don't care how bad you smell. You're here." She grinned; it was clear she had jumped out of bed to greet him.

"I care," Chad joked. He ran his hand over his head.

Hope shook her head. "What can I get you? Water? Coffee? Beer?" She was eagerly pacing her way to the kitchen.

Chad walked up behind her and redirected her back to the bedroom. "I want you to get back into bed. I will shower, and join you when I'm done. We'll catch up and cuddle."

He was exhausted, and as much as he wanted to pull her into the shower and make passionate love to her, his body could not handle it right now. What he wanted to do right now was to wash the smells of the field off, and fall asleep wrapping his arms around his girl.

After tucking Hope back into bed, he pressed a kiss to her cheek and forehead, and made his way to the shower.

He stripped his utilities off, and stepped into the steady stream. There was nothing more blissful than the hot water on his skin. He took his time scrubbing his body, then lingered under the hot water, just for the extra rinse, before shutting the water off. He was eager to curl up next to his Hope, smelling her scent all night.

He stepped out of the shower, and wrapped a towel around his waist. Chad smiled, seeing Hope's petite shape already asleep in bed, her body curled up under the covers, facing the shower as if she was awaiting his arrival, but her body succumbed to the late hour. He quietly dried off and slipped on his boxer briefs before climbing into bed. Chad hated disturbing Hope's sleeping form, but nothing was more satisfying after a hot shower than feeling her body against his.

"Shhh. It's just me. Go back to sleep." He comforted her disrupted self and stroked her arm. He wrapped his body around hers and slid his arm under her head, nuzzling his face into her hair, his preferred position to sleep with her.

That night was the best night of sleep Chad had in the last six weeks. He woke up with Hope cradled under his arm as he slept on his back. He couldn't get over how perfect she felt against him. There was nothing he could compare this moment to, but bliss. He smiled as she stirred, stroking his thumb over her temple.

Her eyes fluttered open. "Good morning, love," she said, turning and wrapping her arm around his bare chest.

"Good morning, gorgeous," he responded, snuggling down and holding her closer.

"Thank you for surprising me last night." Hope was talking with her eyes closed, as if she were still sleeping.

"I couldn't go home knowing I would miss out on a night of being with you." This was a new level of sappiness that was coming out, but Chad didn't care.

"I am glad you did. I texted Lulu that you came home early. Em is covering me today," Hope added casually.

"Really? You have the day off?" Chad rolled over to his side and wrapped his arm around her waist, pulling her to himself. "We can just lay here all day and catch up?"

Hope smiled at Chad. Not hesitating with morning breath, she cupped his face in her hands, stroked his cheeks like he did hers, and pressed her lips against his. The kiss was brief and sweet. "Yes. We can do whatever you want today. When do you have to go back to work?" Hope traced over the outline of Chad's face. He knew the sun wasn't kind to his skin, no matter how much sunscreen he put on, he always darkened and burned. His face showed the outlines of his sunglasses and helmet.

"Good. Because that is all I want to do. Lay right here and talk to you. I don't have to go back until Monday. I have a 72." Chad snuggled his face into her neck and hair.

"I have three days with you?" Hope squealed with delight.

"Yes, all three days with you." Chad sat up now, with his head in his hand. "So, what did you do these last six weeks?" He traced his fingertips over the skin of her upper arm, knowing how much she liked that.

Hope purred softly before replying, "After I got over the fact that you literally had no form of communication with me, I wrote. I started writing the Paisleys' story. Actually, I'm really close to finishing. I told them about it, and you should've seen them, Chad! They were so amused by the fact I wanted to write their story through my eyes."

Chad leaned forward and pressed an affectionate kiss

behind her shoulder. "I am so proud of you for writing. Will you let me read it?"

Hope laughed at the tickle of his kiss, leaning back and bringing her arm up and around his neck in a loose hold. "You want to be one of my beta readers?"

"What's a beta reader?" Chad said, amused by her playful wrestling move.

Hope turned around to face him, placing her head on his chest. "Well, a beta reader is someone who reads a book after the author finishes a draft and self-revises it. Sometimes they read it before the editor looks at it, sometimes they see it after the editor. I like when the betas read it before, though, so I can send the cleanest version to the editor."

"Well I would love to read it and give you feedback. I am not sure how helpful I'll be, though." Chad cradled her head against his chest, his fingers tangling into her hair, and stroking it out.

"Well, just tell me what you think when I'm done?" Hope peeked up at him. Chad loved her hazel eyes, the shape of her face, and the way her hair wisped around the outline of her face.

"Absolutely. How is your Dad? Harper?" He stroked her hair, nuzzling her face to his. He relished being able to catch up with her.

"Dad's doing well. Apparently, he's lost forty pounds, and is getting super fit. Actually…" Hope sat up now, facing him, her knees tucked underneath her. She set her hands on his chest and abdomen. "They're coming in two weeks to visit. Harper will stay with me for a few weeks, and Dad will be here for the weekend he drops her off and for a few extra days when he comes to pick her up."

Chad smiled at Hope's encouraged voice. He had

witnessed the growth that Hope had experienced. Her grief was changing; he could tell she was rising out of the ashes of her tragedy, and he was proud to be there to watch. "Well, I look forward to seeing them. What does Harper like to do?"

Hope smiled, leaning over and pressing a kiss on his lips before sitting back on her bottom. "You're so sweet. She likes to read, listen to music, paint, go to the movies..." Hope sat back and thought for a moment. "She'll like you."

Chad smiled at the ending of her comment. "How do you know that? How will Dad take me?" He poked her thigh, teasing her.

"I think you and Dad will get along just fine, but you probably shouldn't sleep over when Dad is staying here. He may take that the wrong way. He sometimes has a streak of old-fashioned judgment." Hope patted his abdomen playfully.

"That's fine, but what about Harper?" Chad ran his hand over her leg just as playfully.

"She'll be fine. The door has to be closed, though." She motioned toward her bedroom door as if Harper was already here.

"Not a problem there. Want coffee?" Chad slowly rose into a sitting position with his back against the headboard, stretching his arms up before resting them in his lap lazily.

"Always." Hope crawled over Chad's legs and slid off the bed, and walked into the kitchen. It only took a few moments before he heard the sound of the grinder, and the water boiling. Not long after, the wonderful aroma of coffee began to waft back into the bedroom.

Chad slid off the bed, grabbed his jersey shorts, and

made his way to the bathroom. He washed his face, rinsed his mouth with the mouthwash Hope had on her counter, and was drying his face when he felt the familiar arms of his girl around his waist. "Well, hi there." He dropped an arm around her shoulder.

"I need you to leave so I can brush my teeth." She grinned up at him.

"You won't let me watch you brush your teeth?" Chad teased her. "I can come up with some dirty references when it comes to toothbrushes and foamed up toothpaste." He grinned back at her, winking as he made his way out of the bathroom.

"And that's why I won't let you watch, goofball," she laughed as she shut the door.

Chad shook his head as he made his way to the kitchen. He pulled two large mugs from the cupboard and poured two cups of coffee. He smiled seeing the glass sugar container next to her coffeemaker. The only reason why she had it out was for him. He poured his preferred amount of sugar into his coffee, stirring it with a teaspoon. Chad carried the mugs to the table and chairs and set the mugs down, and returned to the kitchen to sift through her cupboards and fridge for breakfast.

Chad pulled the carton of eggs, shredded cheese, and the loaf of bread Hope kept in the refrigerator. "What are you doing?" Hope asked, smacking his bottom as she walked into the kitchen.

"Making us grub." Chad crinkled his nose playfully at her.

"Can I take over?" Hope leaned against the counter.

"Nope." Chad cracked the eggs into the hot pan. "I haven't cooked in six weeks," as if he truly missed cooking.

Hope laughed, seeing straight through his sham reasoning. "Oh? Okay, but I get to clean up. So... I'll just be over here, drinking my coffee." She swayed her way to the table and chairs, in complete line of sight of the kitchen. She sat down, extending her legs out on the chair across from her, teasing him with her cup of coffee.

Chad shook his head as he pulled two plates from the cupboard. When the eggs were perfectly cooked, he layered a thick layer of cheese on them, waiting for it to melt before sliding them on the plate. Chad pulled two slices of toast for each plate from the toaster.

He nodded, proud of his last-minute creation. He headed to the table, setting a plate in front of Hope and then one in front of his. He smiled at her, leaning over to give her a peck on the nose before he sat back in his chair.

Chad's stomach grumbled, protesting the long hours of fasting he sustained.

"Well, Chad, you better eat or your stomach is going to get up and leave your body," she grinned as she cut into her eggs.

He shook his head at her. "I'll live. How are the eggs?" Chad waited for her assessment before cutting into his own.

Hope's response was a mumbled moan of delicious-ness. She lifted a piece on her fork and toasted him in the air. Chad laughed, still shaking his head.

"I guess that's a good sign. I didn't lose my egg touch." He leaned over his own plate to begin eating. As usual, Chad and Hope ate in quiet, simply enjoying their food and each other's company. It was their unique trait; their sacred time together.

Chad finished before Hope, like any typical meal. He pushed his plate aside, wiped his face with a napkin, and watched her take the last few bites of her breakfast. He peeked into his empty mug, setting it back on the table.

Hope wiped her face, smiling at him as he watched his empty mug. "Thank you for cooking this morning. It was delicious. Need a refill on coffee?"

Chad, surprisingly, shook his head. "Nah, I'm good. Maybe in an hour or two. I think I'm full." He nodded with satisfaction.

Chad attempted to grab Hope's plate, but she swatted at his hand. "No! I'm cleaning remember?" she chided him, grinning as she stood.

He lifted his hands up innocently. "Fine, fine. I won't stop you. If washing dishes is your thing, then go for it, dollface." He wrapped his arm around her waist when he stood, and pulled her down to his level to press a tingle-inducing kiss against her lips before releasing her.

Chad felt flat. He struggled to stay awake, watching Hope wash the dishes from his seat before he rose. Maybe he should have another cup of coffee. No, he probably should lay down a bit longer. He ran his hand over his face. Chad entered the kitchen, grazing his hand on Hope's lower back. "I'm still super tired. I'm really sorry for dragging this morning."

Hope turned the water off, and dried her hands on the towel hanging on the cupboard towel bar. She turned and wrapped her arms around his waist. His arms languidly circled around her as they rocked silently in the kitchen for a brief moment. "Training wiped you out, huh?" Hope's hands linked together, closing Chad in her embrace.

"It has a tendency to do that. It takes a day or two to get back to normal sometimes. Mind if we just have a lazy day today?" He leaned down and pressed his face against her hair.

"Absolutely. I'll write while you sleep, and maybe join you in napping." Her sweet compassion warmed Chad up. He was concerned she would want to hit the ground running and honestly, the last thing he wanted to do was to be out and about. Chad was glad Hope was on board with the plan.

Chad felt Hope release him, and patted him on his hip affectionately. "Go lie down. I'll join you with my laptop."

He pressed an appreciative kiss against her temple, squeezing her once more before heading toward her bedroom. He sprawled himself on her bed, hugging a pillow under an arm and his head, as he tried to sleep on his side. Hope was in the front of his mind, as always. She was kind, compassionate, and strong-spirited. She was overcoming one of life's most challenging experiences of losing a parent, let alone losing her mom traumatically. He smiled to himself. Her tenacity was a turn on and he admired her.

A wave of guilt washed over him. He meant to express his feelings to her before training, and although he expressed his feelings in their physical act of intimacy, he never followed through with those cherished words. He needed to find the right time to tell her he cared for her, that he loved her. He loved her more than he could admit.

It wasn't long before the bed pressed downward, as Hope slide into bed with him. He heard her rustling and settling her laptop on her nightstand before sliding down further and scooting her way to him. He naturally held her close, kissing the back of her head.

"Thank you for understanding," he whispered into her hair.

She patted his arm tenderly. "It's okay. I just want you to be here."

He stroked her hair out of her face, taking her into his memory for those late nights on base. "Hope?"

"Hmmm?" Hope responded, her eyes closed.

Chad wrapped himself around her, and summoned the courage to share his feelings with her. "I love you."

chapter *eleven*

HOPE

"*I* LOVE YOU," CHAD WHISPERED in her ear. Her heart stopped for a pregnant pause. She turned around and faced him, caressing his cheek, as if she was looking for confirmation of what he just said. Chad repeated himself. "I love you, Hope. I wanted to tell you the night before I left for training, but I was a coward."

"Shhhh." Hope placed a finger over Chad's lips. "Stop. You did. You showed me how much you loved me." Hope continued to stroke his face as she searched his eyes, her mind overwhelmed with words and emotions. "I love you too." Her eyes brimmed with tears, the emotions taking over. She felt intensely stupid for crying.

Chad chuckled pulling her close, kissing her eyes. "Why in the world are you crying? Do you regret loving this oaf?" His self-deprecating humor making Hope laugh through her tears.

"No, of course not. I just... I just think that... that you're the sweetest, kindest man I've ever met, and I can't believe I get to call you mine," Hope laughed through her tears. "I'm pathetic, don't mind me."

Chad chuckled as he held her to his chest, stroking her

back. "I feel the same about you, baby. Do you need me to cry?" He winked.

"No." Hope wiped her face with her hands, resting her head on his chest. "But would you if I said yes?" She grinned up at him playfully.

"I would try really hard, but I don't think I can guarantee success." Chad leaned forward and kissed Hope's head. "I think I would do anything to make you happy, though."

Hope's heart fluttered at his words; she felt his sincerity to her bones. "I think the feeling is mutual, Chad." She scooted upward so she was eye to eye with him.

He held her face in his hands, staring into her mesmerizing hazel eyes. His strength, his masculinity, and his protectiveness exuded from how he held her in moments like these, and Hope cherished it. Chad pressed his lips against hers. It was soft, and sweet, and it turned Hope's insides upside down. She moaned softly into the kiss.

"I want you," Chad rumbled as he pulled Hope beneath him. He hovered over her, and Hope melted under him. She could spend her eternity just like this, with all these feelings. He leaned inward, as if there were others around them. "Condom?"

Hope grinned at his question, and pointed toward the nightstand drawer. "I put them where you put yours."

Chad chuckled, and pressed a kiss on her nose as he stretched his upper body over to the drawer, digging with his fingers to find the foil. Hope stroked Chad's sides and abdomen, absorbing the muscle lines that framed his body. He was so beautiful.

When he repositioned himself over her, she took the foiled square in her own hand. Chad looked surprised by the action, but she placed a finger on his mouth to prevent a protest. "I'm doing it this time."

Chad raised a brow but didn't protest. He settled his weight over her, staring her down, it was if he was trying to decide where to start. Hope bent a knee and rested it against the outside of his hip. Her fingers traced his lower abdomen and moved upward, and Chad kissed her again, but this time with a rougher, deeper, and more hungry drive. She felt his intensity as his tongue dipped to meet hers.

Her hands wrapped around his hips, gripping his strong body with equal desire, breaking their kiss, breathless. "I want to be on top," she stated before kissing him again, a hand sliding up to rest on his face tenderly.

He growled at her suggestion. He did it often when they were intimate and it drove her wild. Hope felt him shift, taking her with him, and in a swift movement, their roles reversed. She found herself straddled on his hips and he was flat on his back. She grinded her hips against his, and he tentatively placed his hands on her thighs. "Easy there, cowgirl, you may wake a dragon you're not quite ready for," Chad teased her as he tugged on the bottom of her shirt to pull her down.

Hope laughed softly at his warning. Removing her shirt, she tossed it to the side of the bed, followed closely by her soft cotton bra. "You're topless, it would only be fair, right?" She leaned over him, and his hands reached up and met her flesh. He caressed and molded her breasts in his hands as they kissed, his soft moans an affirmative response.

He broke their kiss to come up for air. "Fuck, woman." He pulled her back down, but brought his lips to one of her soft mounds, taking in one of her nipples, suckling. He teased her, circling it with his tongue before letting it pop out of his mouth. He paid the same attention to the other side. Hope's arousal was now far greater than what she could wait for.

She hooked her hands around the band of her shorts and wiggled out of them. She gripped Chad's waistband of his shorts and boxer briefs and pulled them down to below his mid-thigh. He kicked them off before Hope lowered herself over his hips. She trapped his growing cock between them, rocking her hips just enough to tease him. His groan was the answer she was looking for, his hands squeezing her upper thighs, telling her to keep going.

Hope diligently reached for the square foil and deftly slid the rubber cover over his erect penis. Her hand then gently cupped his balls and she squeezed him ever so gently, smiling when his upper thighs tightened, followed by a low growl.

Hope slid her palm over the bottom length of his cock, before she glided around the base, angling him upward toward her hips. Hope watched his face as she lowered herself onto him. His hands around her hips slowed her descent even more, as she reveled in how he felt inside of her.

His girth and thickness stretched at her inner walls, and she rocked her hips to accommodate him. When they were perfectly fit, Hope began to move slowly, short yet deep thrusts, their height difference forcing her to press her hands against his chest for leverage. They shared in soft moans as they connected together.

Hope began to feel him drive upward, increasing the speed and momentum of their shared thrusts. His hands slid to her ass, cupping each cheek. She allowed him to take over, directing the speed, as she pushed down to meet him. Her upper body swayed over the top of his, her breasts bouncing to the rhythm of his hips.

The temptation of her breasts hovering over his face and mouth was too much for Chad, and it was fully intentional on Hope's part. He rose to meet them, taking a full mouthful of each breast, first one and then the other. He nuzzled his face into her flesh. Her soft whimpers and her inner thighs tightening around his hips were cues that she was nearing her climax.

Chad shifted his weight and braced himself against the headboard in a half-sitting position. Hope felt him grip her hips like a vice; his thrusts were long, fast, and deep. Her body going for the ride he was giving her, when her first intention was to pleasure him. She wrapped her arms around his neck. Their lips locked together, and his arm drifted upward to hold her head in the kiss, before he broke it to demand her orgasm.

"Give it to me. Let go." His voice was gruff, and raspy, as he thrust hard into her, bracing her body against his hips with one hand, her head in a kiss with the other. Chad was stealing her breath as climax overwhelmed her system. Her body tremored and convulsed as Chad continued to drive into her, and she screamed out his name through her release.

Hope felt Chad ride her climax out, before adding his own to the mix, which brought Hope's pleasure to a new intensity. Chad gripped her hips and slid himself as deep as he could before arching his back against the headboard. Hope cradled his head against her chest as they shared in the intimate moment together.

Hope stroked his sides as Chad slowly relaxed against the headboard, holding his Hope against his body. She tenderly kissed the front of his shoulder, then looked into his eyes. "I was supposed to lead that one." Hope leaned in and pressed a soft kiss on his lips. "You're tired, and I didn't want to have to make you work." She rested her head on his shoulder. "But I wouldn't change anything at all."

Chad's embrace tightened around her. Hope's body proportionally fit over his, perfectly, like puzzle pieces. Chad waited for a moment before responding to her soliloquy about their love-making session. With a half-chuckle, he ran his fingers through her hair and stroked her scalp tenderly, sending slow shivers down Hope's spine.

"Baby, I don't care how we do it, but I certainly wouldn't change anything either."

Hope cherished these few moments, their sweaty bodies melding, running the high of the endorphins together.

It was Chad that broke the moment this time. Hope felt a sweet kiss at the top of her head. "I'm going to clean up. Stay here, please?"

Hope wasn't going to refuse that request, as she shifted off his body, freeing him to stand.

"I'm not going anywhere." Hope laid on her stomach, sliding her arms around a pillow, hugging it to her body.

"Good." Chad turned and winked at her. She smiled at the wrinkle at his eyes. He was so distinguished and content in his own skin. That had to be a military thing, maybe. She found her comfortable place in the sheets, waiting for his return. Chad opened the bathroom door after cleaning up. He rubbed his hands as he walked to the bed, lifted the covers, and slid his body back into the cocoon.

Hope smiled as she felt Chad find his position around her and rest his face in her hair. It was something unique he did. She never had anyone do that with her. It was endearing. He rested a hand over her head possessively, and she listened as his breathing became slower, and more regular, as he fell asleep. It wasn't much longer that Hope felt herself losing the battle of staying awake. Her eyes fluttered closed, submitting to the impending slumber.

chapter twelve

CHAD

*C*HAD AWOKE TO THE SOFT sound of keyboard keys. He opened his eyes but didn't move. Hope was sitting with her back against the headboard, her laptop balanced in her lap. She was in her writing zone. He momentarily admired the light bouncing off her face as she worked diligently on her story before reaching across the space between them where he rested his hand on her upper thigh, smiling at her.

Hope's eyes were diverted from the screen, to his hand and then to him. "Well, hello sleepyhead." Her smile did that funny thing to his heart.

"Hey." His voice was gruff and dry. "How long was I sleeping? What time is it?" He moved closer, into a sitting position next to her. He rested his chin on her shoulder, glancing at her computer screen.

Hope laid her head on his. "You were out for six hours. I didn't have the heart to wake you. You looked so peaceful. It's two o'clock."

Chad laughed. "Yeah, during training, we're in a constant state of sleep deprivation. I'll probably go to sleep at a regular time and sleep through the night." He heard Hope's stomach growl. "We need to get lunch, don't we?"

Hope smiled down at Chad, nodding. "Yeah, it's probably a good idea. I was planning on hitting Piggly Wiggly up after work today, but since I'm not working, want to go with me now? I am sure you need some food at your place too. We can grab some stuff for sandwiches."

"Sure. Let me shower and we can head out." He leaned into Hope's ear, kissing her lobe before whispering, "Join me?"

Hope laughed at his suggestion. "I showered while you slept, but I don't mind helping." She slid her laptop off her lap and onto her nightstand.

Chad feigned a protest as he slid off the bed and headed toward the shower. "You're too productive for your own good."

Hope followed him into the bathroom, where they played and teased each other, then afterward, took turns drying each other off. Chad admired Hope's body as she dressed. She had a naturally athletic figure, but she wasn't a huge gym goer. Hope fit him and that was all that really mattered.

Hope offered to drive, but he wouldn't let her. He grabbed his keys from her counter. When they reached Piggly Wiggly, Chad was put in charge of pushing the cart while Hope darted down the aisles, looking for items. He occasionally placed items in his small side. Hope consulted him about his thoughts on dinner for the week. They typically took turns making dinner for each other, but Hope took over most dinners before training because of his long hours. He planned to change that until the long hours kicked in again before deployment.

Hope and Chad made their way around the store. This

felt right. He didn't want anything to change. He enjoyed her questioning and decision-making. He also loved watching her shoulders lift and drop when she finally made the decision on what she wanted. Hope touched the cart and turned to him. "Done?"

"I'm done," he said. He only needed a few things, as he typically ate on base. They checked out together, their banter on who was going to buy what delayed their exit but they managed to find a happy medium. The gentleman in him hated watching her pay for a meal he would partake in but she was stubborn and independent, so he compromised.

Chad insisted in loading the truck, and he shook his head as he watched her cross the parking aisle to push the cart in the return kiosk. Chad was waiting for her with her passenger side door open. As she grazed his waist, he stole a sweet kiss. "You know I can walk a cart back for us."

Hope laughed as she folded herself into her seat. "Oh, I know. I just like sharing responsibility. You loaded, so I took the cart back."

Chad shrugged his shoulder, shaking his head as he made his way to his side of the truck. As they drove, he asked, "Hope, what do you think of redoing some landscaping before your Dad and sister come?"

"At Lulu's?" she asked, moving her gaze from outside the truck over to him.

"Yes, of course, if she approved. We could hang that porch swing again. It just needs some parts replaced, that we can pick up at Home Depot. Freshen it up on the outside?" he suggested, looking at her.

"You would help me do that? Can I help you do yours, too? Though, it really doesn't need much," Hope mused, her voice pitched higher in anticipation.

"I'd love to, Hope." Chad smiled at her. "I'd like that. We can do it this weekend, if you like. It'll be our weekend project. You just have to check with Lulu, of course."

Hope pulled out her phone and was instantly connected to the older lady that owned the Koffeehaus, and Hope's home. After a brief exchange, Hope looked up at Chad. "She said she would pitch in by taking some off my rent too. She's looking forward to meeting my family."

Chad smiled at her. "I didn't think she would mind. She's a good lady. How about we get home, eat lunch, and do some planning. Then we can head out to Home Depot and Lowe's."

"Wow, Chad. That would be so much fun. I've never really tended to my own landscaping." Hope settled into her seat, reaching over and holding Chad's hand.

Chad squeezed it before teasing her, "I know. It's why I mow and edge your lawn for you."

Chad's heart swelled as she laughed at his response. "Hey! I'm learning."

He chuckled, reaching over and patting her thigh affirmatively. "Yes, yes, you are. I'm impressed you learned how to change your toilet chain. You'll be Ms. Fix It in no time."

Hope shook her head. He took her hand again and intertwined his fingers with hers. She rested her head on the headrest, and he could feel her contentment. It was contagious, because he certainly felt it.

He pulled into her driveway. Together, they carried the groceries inside. After they both got settled, Hope busied herself making them a lunch of deli sandwiches with chips and fruit salad. Chad perused the paper ads for Home Depot and Lowe's, offering ideas as he saw them.

Hope chimed in with her opinion. It was clear she was

most excited about the porch swing than any other part of the landscaping project. He was glad to help her, and they both enjoyed spending time outside. He also had another idea he was going to surprise her with, but that wasn't going to happen until she was busy doing something else.

Hope walked out of the kitchen and placed a plate with a heaping stack of a sub, chips, and a small bowl of fruit salad. She sat next to him with a near matching plate, proud of her creation. "Eat up!"

Chad placed the ads on the table and heartily rubbed his hands together. "This looks awesome. Thank you, Beautiful."

Hope smiled at him, waiting for him to take the first bite before eating. It was a silly tradition they had, he thought, but he enjoyed sharing the silent moment. He lifted his sandwich and took a bite. He gave her a thumbs up and she jumped into her own sandwich. While they ate, Chad asked questions of the types of flowers she thought she could maintain, and what tools she would need. He leaned forward and stole one of her chips. Hope grinned, smacking at his hand playfully. "There's more in the kitchen. Want me to get you some?"

Of course she would offer. He shook his head. "No, I just wanted that one."

"You're silly," she remarked as she took the last bite of her fruit salad. She dusted her hands off over the plate and handed her plate to him as he stood. She didn't protest the cleaning today, which made him smile. As he passed her, he kissed her forehead lightly.

"I made a list of things we need to pick up. Do you want to pick them up today? Or join the masses tomorrow?"

"Let's go today. We can do one house tomorrow and

one house Sunday?" Hope suggested as Chad placed the plates in the sink, and started washing dishes.

"Sounds good. I'll finish these and we can take off?" he replied.

"Okay. I'll be writing until you want to go." She wandered back into the bedroom where she left her laptop last, a little pep in her step.

Chad smiled as he watched her disappear around the corner. He admired her motivation and drive to finish her story. He delayed their departure as long as he could, so she could get plenty of writing time in. It was only after he couldn't delay any longer that he made his way into the bedroom. He laid perpendicular to her, placing his head on her lower legs.

She tilted her laptop down. "Are you ready?" She bounced his head gently, teasing.

"Only if you are, but you can keep writing. It's still pretty early in the day."

She tapped a few keys before closing the laptop. "Let's go. I can write later." She wiggled her legs free and stood from the bed.

He chuckled as he followed her out of the bedroom. He grabbed his keys and wallet off the counter, and opened the front door for Hope.

The ride to the first store included a review of the list - minus his surprise, of course - and plan of action. They decided that they would do his house first, since there wasn't as much to do, then start on Hope's this weekend and, if need be, complete it next weekend. Her dad and sister weren't coming until the following week.

To onlookers, their chemistry was hard to miss. Their rhythm worked like a machine. They were not only a good pair, they were an efficient one. Chad and Hope completed their rounds between the home improvement stores within just a few hours. Chad's truck was filled to the brim with soil, mulch, flowers, and other tools they would need this weekend. Chad had to return later to pick up the surprise he had planned. He was sure she was going to enjoy it. Hope wasn't afraid to get her hands dirty and he loved that about her. It went with her feminine grace. She carried herself in a way that Chad couldn't resist.

chapter *thirteen*

HOPE

A HAMMOCK. CHAD HAD SET up a hammock for Hope in her backyard. And not just any hammock – a deluxe one, that at least three people could fit in comfortably. He had to have planned the distance between the two trees perfectly. Chad knew it was shady throughout the day. Hope swung gently in the wind, taking in the beautiful summer day, with her laptop hugged to her stomach. Hope spent the last few hours writing, waiting for the text from her sister, signaling their arrival into town. Harper had been texting her throughout the road trip, complaining mostly about how Dad was not a fan of her music.

Hope grinned. It had been over a year since she had seen her dad and Harper. She talked to them every week, though, trading photos and texts throughout the week. Dad was well-informed of Chad's presence in her life, and at first was very cautious, but had grown very comfortable with their relationship. Hope believed that her dad and Chad would get along just fine. Chad and Harper? She wasn't sure. It could go either way, but Chad was persistent and kind, and Harper liked kindness. No, Harper thrived on kindness.

Hope's phone pinged with an incoming message, but it wasn't Harper, it was Chad. He was going to be late from work. He was covering a duty shift until 3PM, but apparently the Major hadn't come in yet, and he couldn't leave until she did.

As she walked back to the house, she admired the work she and Chad did to the flower beds in the backyard. She even had potted plants on her screened-in porch. Chad was her landscaping hero. Her mom taught her how to grow plants in pots but she had never planted plants in the ground. Her dad always handled the outside work. Hope loved the way Chad took his time to teach her about each plant, how deep to plant it, and how often to water it. It was two weeks, and the plants and flowers were just taking off.

Hope pulled open the screen door and stepped in. Since Chad wasn't going to be home in time to greet her Dad and sister, she wanted to make sure coffee was brewed and the beer was properly chilled. Singing quietly, she hit the coffeemaker button, expecting her guests any time now. Hope pulled open her refrigerator and saw that Chad had put Corona on the bottom shelf, and added Black Dog Ale next to it for himself. She smiled, loving that he planned to spend time here.

Hope heard the trill tone and lifted her phone up to read a message from her sister.

"ETA - OPEN THE DOOR!"

Hope squealed as she set her phone down, ran to her

door and threw it open to see her Dad pull their familiar red minivan into her driveway. She ran to the van, and before Dad even put it in park, Hope was at the passenger side.

Hope hugged Harper so hard as they rocked side to side for a moment. Hope held her sister out at arm's length to look her over, both in tears. They wiped each other's tears away, giggling. "Dang girl, what have you been eating? You've gotten so tall this year. You're taller than I am!"

Harper laughed through her tears. "Must be Dad's cooking." Harper squeezed Hope one more time before letting Hope see their dad.

Hope ran over to the driver's side when she saw him slide out of his seat. There was nothing holding back her tears now. Hope was near childlike sobs, her shoulders heaving as her father wrapped his arms around her. "Hi, sugar. Why are you crying?" He held her close, comforting her.

Hope didn't know why she was crying, but all she could do was hold her father in her driveway. Harper came in from behind and wrapped her long arms around Hope and her Dad. "It's okay, Hope, we're here," Harper said.

In the middle of the emotional reunion, Chad pulled his truck up to the side of the driveway and stepped out. He was still in his utilities, and he was holding his cover in his hand, curling the shade in his palm. Hope was completely taken by surprise when she saw him walking up the driveway, smiling. He waved and said, "Hey. Major showed up right after we texted."

He walked up with his arm extended out toward her father. "Welcome to Jacksonville, North Carolina, sir. I'm

Chad." Hope's dad, Ben, turned and greeted Chad warmly, taking his hand and patting his shoulder with the other arm.

"Please to meet you, son. Call me Ben. I've heard plenty about you." Hope clasped her hands together, watching the introduction. She wiped her face quickly, still hiccupping from her earlier tears.

Harper, a good three inches taller than Hope, wrapped her arms lazily around Hope's neck, also watching, and whispered in her ear, "I think Dad approves."

Hope couldn't help but laugh, patting her sister's arms affectionately. "I think you're right...maybe." She had to add the hesitancy, because she never knew.

Chad patted Ben's shoulder as he leaned forward and pressed a tender kiss on Hope's wet cheek. "Hi baby, why the tears?" he asked, wiping away stray tears.

Hope shrugged, sliding into a side embrace with him. "I got overwhelmed when I saw them."

Chad stroked the back of Hope's head before sending one of his signature smiles toward Harper. "This must be the beautiful Harper." He reached out his hand to her.

Harper rolled her eyes and moved in to give him a hug. Chad laughed, breaking his side hug with Hope to wrap his arms around her sister.

"Hi, Chad." That was all she could say.

"You guys aren't family, are you?" Chad teased, laughing as he let go of Harper. "Hope likes to hug too."

Chad turned to include Ben in the conversation. Hope recognized how well Chad navigated the potentially awkward situation so gracefully, and it made her embarrassingly turned on.

"Ben, let me grab your bags for you." Chad pulled the

two suitcases out after her father opened the door. "Shall we go in? There's beer chilling in the fridge and I know Hope was toiling over some lasagna today."

Hope led the way in, holding the screen door open so that her dad, sister, and then Chad could walk in. Chad leaned in to sneak a kiss before he stepped in with his hands full.

"Hello again, beautiful," he whispered, so neither guest overheard the over-sappy greeting.

Hope smiled up at him tenderly. He grew more and more handsome as each moment passed. Chad placed the suitcases in the guest room and met them in the family room area. Hope corralled her family outside to the porch to relax on the lounge chairs outside. Chad followed with a cold beer for Ben and himself, and a cold soda for Harper. "If you'll excuse me, I'm going to get out of my uniform." He set his unopened beer on one of the side tables and stepped inside, following Hope back in.

They made it as far as the kitchen, then looked around the corner before sneaking in a sweet tender kiss. Hope wrapped her arms around his waist. "I'm glad you got out early enough."

"Me too. Me too. I was looking forward to meeting them. Glad I got here in time. I'm going to go change. Meet you out there?" He caressed her cheek.

Hope nodded, letting her hand linger around his hip as he left the kitchen. She pulled out her pre-made lasagna and placed it in the oven. Hope set the timer, grabbed a soda from the fridge, and made her way outside. She sat in one of the single chairs across from Ben and Harper.

"Sugar, you have a nice little place here," her dad stated as he drank his Corona. Hope noted that Chad had provided a lime too. She was impressed with his hosting skills.

"Thanks, Dad. It has turned into a super happy place for me," she said. "Chad's helped me really make it mine."

Her dad smiled. "He seems like a nice young man. Are you doing okay?" His voice had that layer of paternal concern.

Harper chimed in, "Dad. Drop it. She looks great, she has a hot boyfriend, and she seems to be getting on pretty well."

Hope nodded. "I *am* okay, Dad. I'm even writing again." She hoped adding that detail would help quell his lingering concern, but it backfired.

"You are?" Her dad was shocked. "Have you approached Gertie?" He was referencing her editor, one of three people she burned on her way out. "What about Lora or Tim?" He just had to mention her other friends. Well, she didn't think they were friends anymore.

"No." Her voice was barely audible. "But I will. I can't write and not making things okay with them. Whether or not I'm extended forgiveness is not something I can control." Hope's voice was about to crack and she broke her dad's eye contact to look down at her soda can.

"Okay," Ben said. She sensed her father study her expression for another moment. "Good girl." Thankfully, he dropped the subject, at least for the time being.

Things went quiet as they tried to recover from the heavy moment, and Hope was relieved when Chad stepped outside to sit with them. She wasn't sure if he read their body language or just walked into the thick air.

"So, how was the drive?" Chad reached for his bottle of beer and popped the top off rather deftly. Hope noticed he was trying to break the tension by redirecting whatever conversation he wasn't a part of.

Ben was the first to respond. "I learned that Florida does not have the worst drivers after all." He laughed heartily at his own response. Hope was relieved he wasn't going to settle on the former conversation and had to laugh quietly at his response.

"Well, who do you think has the worst?" Chad mused, taking a sip of his beer, resting his head on his hand.

"Georgia. Georgia has the worst drivers." Ben set his beer down.

Harper groaned, slapping her forehead with her hand, shaking her head. "Please, Dad, please don't go into this."

Hope laughed but didn't add to the conversation. Chad piped in for her, probably sensing her lingering unease, "Sorry Harper, I really want to know."

Ben leaned forward onto his knees. He had his hands out, demonstrating the car movements with such eagerness, you would think it had just happened and not five hours prior. By the end of the demonstration and explanation, Chad was about to fall off his chair laughing. Hope had tears streaking down her face from how hard she laughed, and Harper was curled up in her chair, feigning disgust, but her body shaking and shuddering, giving her laughter away.

Hope checked her watch and jumped up. "I need to uncover the lasagna. Anyone need refills?"

"I'll take another, honey," Ben responded, his eyes soft, and she sensed he was trying to gauge where they stood.

"No problem, Dad." Hope gave him a small smile and nod, reassuring him it was okay. "Chad, Harper?" She looked at them.

Harper shook her head, lifting her can. "I still have some."

Chad shook his head, lifting his partially-filled bottle. "I'll have another over dinner. Thanks, babe."

Hope escaped into her home, the aroma of cheese, garlic, and Italian seasoning beginning to fill the room. She smiled as she made her way to the kitchen. Hope uncovered the lasagna and layered a final layer of cheese on the top, and placed it back in the oven. Hope cut the long Italian bread lengthwise so she could slather the delectable garlic butter she'd made earlier over it. Just as she was finishing, the timer for the lasagna went off. She was really nailing her timing today. She placed the bread on a cookie sheet and swapped the lasagna with it.

She heard the glass door slide open, as she was in the middle of chopping up vegetables for the salad.

"Sugar?" Her dad walked in, leaning on the counter. "I didn't mean to upset you out there earlier."

Hope turned to face her father and smiled. "I know. I just think, maybe, that was my biggest regret in how I dealt with losing Mom. I'm more disappointed in myself than anything. I didn't mean to not pay them. But I also actively didn't. I didn't follow up, and abandoned them when I needed to address the issue professionally. It was insulting not to reach out. I blocked them. I don't know if I could ever return to the indie industry and really, at this point, Chad has shown me that I was meant to write, whether I publish or not."

"He's right. You write because it's what's inside you. If you were meant to publish, you will, but you've got bridges to build again, darling." Her dad had soft eyes; the wrinkles had deepened in the last year. She saw the effects of deep grief on his face, and in his hair. He had lost a lot of hair and he was much more gray.

Hope placed her knife down, shaking her head. The sudden surge of grief was brimming to the surface. She covered her mouth and her eyes with one hand as she started talking, her knuckles on the other white from gripping the edge of the counter. "I miss her, Dad. I miss her so much."

Her Dad rushed to her side, wrapping her in his arms. His paternal love comforted her the only way a parent could.

"I miss her too, sweetheart. I miss her every day, every hour, and every minute of my life. It's okay to miss her. She loved big and she loved hard, so when we lost her, that loss was huge." Her father was crying now as well, and he held her head to his chest as they shared the moment, his warm tears trickling over her hair. His vulnerability comforted her in ways she couldn't explain. "You were acting out in grief. What we do in grief never makes sense. But I am so proud of you right now. I was worried I was going to come to find you without a job, downtrodden, and in dire need of your mother. What I see is a grown woman, a woman who draws from the strengths of her mother and pulls through the obstacles of life. You have a beautiful life here. You even have an upstanding boyfriend." He winked, squeezing her shoulder affectionately. "Hope Madison Garner, you are a reflection of your mother. You did not run away. You found a way to heal when no one thought you could. If it means you have to be away from us, then let it be. What I hear right now is not grief; what I hear, sugar, is you haven't forgiven yourself. You haven't forgiven yourself about that night, and you haven't forgiven yourself on how you grieved."

Hope wept on her father's shoulder as he cradled her. "How do I do that, Dad? I hate feeling this way." Her father pushed her out to arm's length, looking at her eye to eye.

"You do what you're doing, love. You live. You live with your mother's spirit inside of you. Every day you get up, dust yourself off, and you keep pushing forward." He stroked her face affectionately. "And you write."

chapter
fourteen

CHAD

*C*HAD PACED HIS HOUSE NERVOUSLY, running his hand over his head. This was unlike him. Chad asked for Ben to stop at his home before he left town for his two-week trip with his bowling buddies. The weekend couldn't have gone any better. He felt confident that he made a very good impression with him. He wasn't afraid to face a General in a briefing, so why was he afraid to talk to his girlfriend's father? He knew why. It was because of what he wanted to ask him.

The doorbell rang. Chad's heart stopped, or at least he thought it did. He walked to the door, took a deep breath, and opened it. There he stood, a tall, wide-statured man; his hair graying but his crystal blue eyes were warm and friendly.

"Hello, Chad. Thank you for inviting me over."

"It really is my pleasure." Chad's mouth felt like it was filled with cotton balls. "Please come in." Chad stepped back to allow Ben to walk in, and led him to his family room. He had spent the last several hours cleaning and vacuuming. Hope helped keep his home clean, but he never let it get dirty. He insisted that it was perfect when Ben came over. "Make yourself comfortable. Can I get you something cold to drink? Beer? Coke?"

Ben took a seat in the single armchair seat. "A nice glass of ice water would be wonderful. Thank you, son."

Words of endearment he used them often, but over the weekend, he only noticed them for his girls. Every once in awhile he'd use them with him. "Got it." He chided himself, *Got it? Really? Don't screw this up*.

Chad walked into his kitchen and poured Ben a large glass of ice water. He pulled a can of Mountain Dew out for himself and walked into his sitting room.

Chad took a seat on the couch, catty-corner from Ben, who broke the silence.

"You asked me to come over to talk about something. What did you need to talk about?" His voice was warm and reassuring.

Chad absentmindedly opened the can of soda, looking at the older man. He had never been so nervous in his life. "Ben, no, Mr. Garner…"

"Ben. Just spit it out." He was amused watching Chad stumbling over his words.

"I love your daughter." Chad blurted out, looking at Ben's face, trying to read his reaction.

Ben leaned forward as he nodded. "I see that, and I deeply appreciate your fondness for her. In fact, I credit your presence in her life as the reason why she's thriving."

Chad shook his head. "No, she deserves all the credit for that. I didn't do anything, but I do love her. I love her more than any other person in this world." Ben nodded, remaining silent. It was clear to Chad that Ben wanted him to continue. "I want to marry your daughter, and I'm asking for your permission."

Ben sat back in the chair, holding the glass of water to his chest briefly. His warm eyes studied Chad. Studied him hard. It felt like an eternity before Ben broke his silence again.

"You love her. But you'll need to leave her for long periods of time. Can you remain faithful?"

"There is no question, sir. Every bone in my body will remain faithful to her. I will never betray her. I may need to deploy or be gone for training, but I will never betray her," Chad insisted.

"What happens if something happens to you?" Ben continued to study him. Chad ran his hand over his scalp nervously. "Chad. I love my daughter more than you. Trust me, I do. I want to ensure that the person who wants to marry her will protect her like I do."

Chad met Ben's gaze, and confidently stated, "I will cross this world to prevent her from hurting. I will lay down my own life to make sure she's safe. I will pay whatever cost to ensure she remains happy. When I was away for six weeks, all I could think about was what I would do when I saw her next. I have her face memorized. Her scent makes me drunk. I would do anything for Hope. Anything."

Ben smiled, leaning over and patting Chad's knee. "Son, that's what I wanted to hear. You have my blessing."

Chad ran his hand over his head as he grinned. His face was lit with excitement. "Thank you, sir, you have no idea how much this means to me."

Ben laughed. "Yes, I do. I remember when I asked Tina's parents for her hand in marriage. I thought I was going to melt into the wall. You did well."

Chad laughed nervously, finally releasing the breath he was holding, "I have another request. It's a bit of a reach, but I'm deploying very soon. Hope doesn't have any leverage as a girlfriend or a fiancée. I would like to marry her at the courthouse before I leave." Chad paused, and rushed to continue before Ben could object. "I promise to give Hope the wedding she deserves when I come back. Wherever, whenever, whatever you guys want. I want Hope to be able to reach me in case of emergencies, and likewise, if I need to reach her. God forbid, if something happens to me, she doesn't have any rights to knowing anything. I want her to have that. It will also give her access to healthcare and other benefits." Chad stopped, needing to hear what Ben thought.

"Well. It isn't exactly ideal. When were you thinking about doing this? You're going to need witnesses. Harper and I would like to be present, of course." Ben looked at him, his eyes still twinkling.

"Well, I was thinking… when you came to pick up Harper in two weeks." His voice was soft; he knew it was a long shot.

"You know what? That isn't a bad idea." Ben nodded, smiling at him. "But she'll have her traditional wedding when you come back. Don't you think about skipping it. Her mother will roll in her grave and haunt me in my dreams if she doesn't."

Chad couldn't help but laugh; Ben was so easygoing. "Sir, you do realize that this is all dependent on one thing, right?"

Ben looked at him for a moment. "Oh?"

Chad nodded. "Hope has to say yes."

HARPER WAS IN ON CHAD'S plan. She was a clever girl. He liked Harper a lot. In fact, he owed Harper a great deal for distracting Hope long enough so he could set up what he wanted to do. Her morning began with a post-it on her coffee mug, and he put together an all-morning and early afternoon scavenger hunt throughout town. Every location was significant. They were either firsts, or favorites, and he left enough cash for Harper to share something with her at each place. He asked her to take a picture if it was a non-business place, like the park where they took their first hike. Harper was responsible for keeping Hope on track and to not give up. Chad was responsible for holding himself together for when she walked through the glass doors.

He sat on the edge of the hammock, rocking back and forth, neurotically checking his watch and his phone. Harper texted sporadically on their adventure to keep him in the loop. Then came the text he was waiting for; they were pulling into the driveway. He stood from the hammock, straightening his black dress uniform jacket and pleated white pants. He moved to the center of the yard, waiting for her to enter the screened-in porch. The female sound of laughter filled the house as they stumbled onto the porch, and then it went silent.

Hope pushed the screen door open. "Chad?" She walked slowly to him while Chad stayed completely still. He could face combat with no fear, but when he faced his potential future wife, he had to steady his breath and quell the pounding of his heart.

Hope stopped short. "Chad, what the are you doing?" Chad couldn't keep a straight face, and he laughed. He laughed so much that Hope joined in. Hope stepped closer for a kiss, lingering for a moment.

He held Hope by the shoulders. "Hope." He wiped his

face with his hand. "You have been one of the most life-changing people I have ever met in my life. You have changed me to be a better man, a better leader, and a better Marine. The only thing that's left for you to challenge me is in one role." He took a deep breath and wiped his face once more, before reaching into his pocket. He pulled out a small black velvet box and lowered down to one knee. "Before your Dad left for his trip, I asked him to come talk to me. With his blessing, I want to know… will you make me the happiest man alive and marry me?"

chapter *fifteen*

HOPE

*H*OPE WAS COMPLETELY STUNNED. HERE, the love of her life, dressed in the most regal, and admirable uniform was kneeling in front of her with a ring in a box. Her hands covered her mouth, and it felt like an eternity before she could breathe, before she could give an answer. She had a million questions, but he only needed an answer to one. The fear etched in his eyes and forehead tipped her over the edge before she gasped out, "Yes," and then again, just in case she wasn't heard, "Yes, yes, yes, yes, yes!"

Chad rose to a standing position, sliding the ring on her finger. He placed his hands on her face, stroking her temples with his thumbs, just the way she loved it. He pressed his soft lips to hers, locking her to him, securing their first engaged kiss with passion that made her heart do flips. He broke the kiss, his face framed with an ear-to-ear grin, his eyes twinkling. The princess cut diamond sat on a double-layered diamond band. Hope held out her hand to look at the prized gem, her mouth partly open. "Chad." She was rendered speechless.

Chad wrapped his arms around her, bringing her to his body. "You're going to be mine, forever."

Hope laughed at his words, and wrapped her arms around his neck, replying, "You do realize that you're going to be *mine* forever."

Their moment was interrupted by Harper. "Eww, guys, go get a room." Harper stood approximately ten feet away, her phone held up at eye-level. "Wave guys, Dad saw everything. I video chatted him."

Hope grinned at the phone, waving feverishly. "Hi, Dad! How could you keep this from me?" She ran to stand next to Harper, dragging her uniformed prince behind her.

There was Ben, with tear-filled eyes. He waved at all three of them. "Honey, why would I tell you this?"

"I don't know, I just can't believe it." Hope wrapped her arms around Chad, as he waved at Ben through the phone.

Ben spoke loudly. "Let me see the ring, sugar. Chad, son, did you tell her what you wanted to do?"

Hope presented her ring to the camera, wiggling her fingers while turning to Chad. "What is he talking about?"

Chad laughed nervously. "Well no, sir, I hadn't told her yet."

Ben chuckled. "Son, what are you waiting for? Don't you know the girls take forever to perfect their plans?"

Hope grabbed his sleeve. "What plans? What do you want to do?"

Chad wiped the sweat off his face. "Let's go inside. It's blazing outside in this uniform."

Hope playfully smacked his arm. "Stop delaying, and tell me."

"I will, I promise." Chad winked at her and motioned for her and Harper to follow him inside. Hope took his hand in hers, and cherished how he felt against her palm. She was preparing her mind for the six months they would soon be apart.

Chad sat her down on the couch, and took a seat beside her. "So, you know I'm going on deployment in just a few months." Hope nodded, waiting with bated breath for him to continue. "I promise you, Hope, that when I get back, we'll have whatever kind of wedding you want. Whatever you've fantasized, we'll do."

This provoked a giggle from Harper. "She never fantasized about her wedding. She did write about them, though."

Hope playfully reached over to smack her sister's legs. "Stop that." She turned back to Chad. "What are you implying? Just spit it out already."

"So, when your dad comes back to pick up Harper, I want to take you to the courthouse to get married. I want you as my wife before I leave. I want you to have access to things you wouldn't have access to as a girlfriend or fiancée." Chad was pleading now, rationalizing every reason.

"What you're saying is, you want to get married in a few days?" Hope reached for Chad's hand, looking for confirmation.

"Yes, yes, that's what I'm saying."

"I get to be Mrs. Turner sooner than later?" Hope pressed a tender kiss against his cheek. "I said yes once, and I will say yes again. Let's get *married*!"

Chad scooped her up into a hug. "You just made me the happiest man alive."

Hope laughed. "Well I thought I did that when I said 'yes' outside." She touched her lips to his, but reigned her affection in since she had an audience.

"You did." He smiled, hugging her in his lap. "We should probably let your dad go back to his bowling." He leaned into her neck, whispering, "You have a wedding to plan for."

Hope grinned at Chad, patting his face affectionately. She turned to Harper and her dad via phone. "Dad, thank you for everything. I can't wait to see you!"

Harper ended the call and put her phone down, and pounced to where Hope and Chad sat. She wrapped her arms around both of their necks simultaneously, awkwardly, yet still at the same time. "I can't wait for Saturday. Sis, we have to go dress shopping, and get your nails done."

Hope laughed, shaking her head, swatting at her sister. "You rascal, hiding this from me. Here I thought I had a confidant who would tell me everything."

Harper stood with her hand on her hip, wagging her finger at her. "You wouldn't have been happy to find this out. It wouldn't have been nearly as fun. And plus, it was too much fun to plan with Chad. I think he kinda likes you." She grabbed her phone, and pranced and danced her way to the guest room. "If you need me, I'll be on Pinterest." She waggled her eyebrows at them as she disappeared down the hallway.

Hope laughed helplessly against Chad's chest. "She is hopeless." She turned to straddle him on the couch, and admire his regalia. The uniform framed his body perfectly. Hope traced the lines of the jacket.

"Your sister is a hopeless romantic. I know someone just like her," he teased, raising his hand to caress Hope's cheek. She smiled at him. "We're getting married, dollface."

"Yes, yes, we're getting married. We are going to be

together, forever." Hope pressed her lips against his. He framed her face with his hands as he dipped his tongue inward. Hope shivered with delight. She loved when he did that.

"We can't do this in front of your sister. Behave, little minx." He swatted her bottom playfully as he stood up. Hope slid off his lap and stood with him.

"So, who is responsible for planning the wedding night?" Hope grinned up at Chad, her eyebrows raised with anticipation.

"Leave that part to me. You do whatever you want for the ceremony, but I claim the night." Chad made his way into her bedroom. "I'm changing clothes. I can't afford to launder this uniform again. Oh, and be prepared, you have some studying to do. You're going to have to take Military Spouse 101 and USMC Officer's Spouse 201 in just a few days."

Hope laughed, shaking her head. "And who is going to be my teacher?

Chad grinned at her as he began to undo his uniform, before the door closed. "Me."

chapter sixteen

CHAD

$\mathcal{C}$HAD SAT OUTSIDE THE COURTHOUSE office with the billet completed. He had paid the order, but Hope and her sister hadn't arrived yet. They couldn't have a ceremony without a second. Ben was there, his hand on Chad's back, playing the reassuring fatherly role; one that was supposed to be reserved for Hope. Chad really liked the old man, and he planned to keep his promises to him when it came to his daughter.

"She's coming, I promise. Harper has her doing some crazy things. You know girls," Ben encouraged, chuckling.

Chad nodded. "Yes, she texted me too. I just can't wait to see her." He took a deep breath and scanned the waiting room, as if she would walk in and sit without greeting him. His eyes caught her familiar form though the glass windows. He rose, straightening his black suit pant legs and jacket. He looked down at his boutonniere one last time to ensure it was perfect. "She's here."

Ben also stood, and Hope walked in, with Harper close behind. She wore a satin cream dress, hugging her body perfectly, the skirt billowing outward to her knees. Hope was beautiful, and graceful, and she was going to be his. Hope waved at the two of them through the security glass. She walked through the metal detectors and wrapped her arms around Chad.

"You look like an angel." Chad leaned over and press a kiss to her lips. "One last one before we get married." He released her so she could greet her father.

"Hello darling, you look stunning." Ben wrapped his arms around his daughter, holding her gingerly. "Your Mom would be in tears right now." Ben wiped his eyes as he took a deep breath.

Harper followed through security. Chad reached out and gave her a fond hug. She was his buddy, the little sister he never had. There were going to be many years of shenanigans, for sure. Hope returned to his side, and he wrapped his arm around her lower back as Harper went to stand with Ben.

Chad looked down at her. "Are you ready? You have only one more chance to escape." He grinned at her, knowing confidently she wouldn't leave.

"I'm ready. Let's do this." Hope squeezed his arm affectionately. "I want to be Mrs. Turner." Chad grinned down at the love of his life and led her to the Clerk of Courts. He slid the receipt for the marriage license to the woman behind the counter. She smiled at the two of them, and directed them and their guests to the little chapel in the room next door, where the clerk would come to marry them.

Chad placed his hand on her lower back, and admired the lace work over her shoulders. He couldn't help himself, and he leaned down to kiss her shoulder. He smiled at Ben and Harper as they made their way to the small chapel room. He felt Hope press back up against his hand. He looked down at her. "You okay?"

Hope bit her lower lip, nodding. "It's so surreal." Her hair was beautifully designed, her sister had braided two chains to the back of her head, and then folded her hair into a bun. She really was stunning.

"Do you need more time?" Chad whispered, afraid the level of concern in his voice may be read as alarmed.

"No, no, no." Hope smiled. They made their way forward to take their spots in the front of the chapel, under the heavily-laced and artificial flowered arch. Ben and Harper had taken their dutiful positions as witnesses in their corner. God, she looked beautiful in the midst of the artificial decorations. He wanted to cherish this moment, but the clerk interrupted his thoughts.

The older woman smiled at the happy couple. "Are you two ready?"

Chad smiled, taking Hope's hands in his. "I'm ready." He looked once more at Hope, tilting his head, letting her have this one last chance to speak up.

Unsurprisingly, Hope grinned, that spectacular bright grin. "Me too."

The clerk smiled and nodded. "Good." She read from a scripted guide in a binder. Their vows were basic, but exactly what Chad and Hope wanted for this "quickie" wedding, as Hope teased him. Chad had already prepared the vows he was going to say at their next ceremony. Ben stepped forward and handed him the ring that matched Hope's engagement band. It came in a set, and was perfect for her.

The ring looked brilliant on her hand, and he was proud for her to wear it. Today, she had taken it off so that he could place the matching diamond band onto her hand. When the clerk cued him to, he slipped the band on her slender finger. Chad didn't think he had stopped smiling since they started exchanging their vows. He watched Hope's face when it was her turn to repeat after the clerk. Her look mirrored his.

She slipped the temporary, yet meaningful, tungsten ring on his hand. She refused to tell him where she found it, but he would cherish this ring, even when the "official" band arrived. His mind was busy - the words ran through his mind, entering one ear literally, and out the other. It wasn't that the vows didn't matter, but it was the fact he was standing in front of his bride, and he was getting married. The man who was married to the Corps, was getting married to the woman of his dreams.

Before he knew it, the clerk of court cued him, "And now you may kiss the bride." Chad looked at the woman and then at Hope.

His smile grew larger. Impossibly, he thought. He cradled her face in his palms gingerly. Hope placed her hands around his waist, and he lowered his lips to hers. Her warm body closed in on his, her arms wrapping around him more tightly. It was the whistle that Harper let out that brought them out of their intimate moment. When Chad opened his eyes, Hope's eyes remained closed. He smiled at her beautiful face, and her attempt to let the moment linger. He whispered to her, "Mrs. Turner."

Hope opened her eyes, studying him closely. "My husband." His arms wrapped around her as he turned, grinning at Ben and Harper who were standing to greet the newlywed couple.

"Well, look at you guys, all lovey dovey. You'd think they just got married or something," Harper joked as she wrapped her long slender arms around Hope's neck, followed by a warm hug for Chad.

Ben was dabbing his eyes with his folded handkerchief. Chad watched Ben kiss his daughter's cheek, letting his embrace linger. When he moved to greet Chad, he extended a hand, wrapping his other arm around him in a tight hug. "Congratulations, son. Thank you for waiting so that we could be here."

He wouldn't have it any other way. Hope's family was her everything. "Thank you, sir." He was going to continue, but the clerk tapped him on the shoulder.

"Sir, you and your wife have to sign your marriage license." She guided Chad and Hope over to a flat surface holding large volumes of books. "You're free to go once you do."

Chad was the first to sign the paper, offering the pen to Hope, stroking her cheek when she took the pen and signed. The woman pressed her seal against the form and signed her own name before making a quick copy, then folding it and handing it to Chad and Hope. "Congratulations."

Ben came up behind them. "The happy couple has some excited guests waiting for them to celebrate at a certain coffeehouse. If we don't hurry, they may drink all the coffee."

Hope looked at her father, back to Chad and Harper, shocked. "Who set that up?"

"Mrs. Lulu. When you told her that you needed today off, and didn't say why, she asked me. You never told me to keep it a secret. She closed the coffee shop just to celebrate." Harper's voice was filled with excitement. Her eyes danced with light, very much like her sister.

Chad reached out and patted Harper's shoulder. "You

really are a sneak. I have a feeling there is more to this than just Mrs. Lulu." He looked at the group and said, "We probably *should* get to Koffeehaus before all the coffee is gone."

Chad couldn't get over Hope's glowing face, her eyes bright. His heart felt like it was going to explode with the amount of love he had for the woman standing next to him. He wrapped his arm around her lower back as they walked toward the exit sign. "Shall we meet you guys there?" It would be their first car ride as a married couple.

Ben nodded, smiling at Chad and his physical signs of devotion toward his daughter. Chad gave Ben a knowing smile, a smile that sent the message he would protect his daughter with every ounce of his being. The group split and as Chad and Hope headed toward his truck, he slid his hand into hers. He would proudly hold this woman's hand forever.

chapter *seventeen*

HOPE

*H*OPE WRAPPED HER ARMS AROUND the petite elderly woman. Mrs. Lulu patted Hope's back fondly. "You and Chad are going to be happy together, forever. Fred and I shared fifty-two years together. The best fifty-two years of my life, I tell you. Cherish each other, forgive often, and always remember that you are each other's number one partner." Mrs. Lulu reached over and pulled Chad into her trademark squeeze.

Hope grinned widely. She admired this woman so much. Mrs. Lulu took those first chances on Hope, and while she owed a lot of her own healing to this woman, this woman's coffee shop was the reason why she met her husband. She would forever be indebted to her.

Hope and Chad had bid Ben and Harper a good night. They were staying at her home, while Chad and Hope spent their wedding night at Chad's home. Chad had originally considered taking Hope on a romantic getaway, but he knew her dad and sister were leaving early the next morning and she would want to see them off. There would be time for romance after Ben and Harper left.

Hope only had a few more weeks with him, and wasn't

sure what she was going to do. He was deploying, and the idea of being physically separated for such an extended amount of time tore her heart to pieces, but this was the life of a Marine Corps wife, and she would get used to it. She had to.

Mrs. Lulu shooed the couple out of the coffeehouse. She insisted that Em and her husband were staying to help her clean up. Harper, Mrs. Lulu, and Em invited mutual friends and favorite customers to the coffeehouse. Even Chad's close friends from base were able to attend, because many of them enjoyed a cup of coffee at Koffeehaus, just like Chad. The modest wedding cake was made by Mrs. Lulu herself. Em completed the beautiful floral decorations and Harper ensured that all the guests were entertained. It was the perfect night. Hope's life was rich with love and she couldn't ask for anything more.

Chad guided Hope outside to the truck, stopping short of Hope's door. Hope looked up at him, unsure why he was hesitating, before he released a jovial laugh. "Those bastards." Hope leaned over to see what he saw and she grinned.

"They love us!" she exclaimed.

It was clear by the military emblems tied to the decorations of his car that it was his friends who doctored his truck up with a sign of "Just Married." Chad shook his head as he pulled Hope's door open. He wrapped his arm around her waist to help her up since she was wearing high heels. "I'll clean it up tomorrow, but let's have fun with it tonight, no?"

"I love it. Definitely keep it for tonight," Chad nodded, grinning up at her.

He closed the door and made his way to his side. He swiftly hoisted himself into the truck. It was only a five-minute drive from Koffeehaus to Chad's home. Hope was in a flirtatious mood now that they were finally alone. She slid her hand into the crook of his elbow as they made their way up his porch, leaning into him, closing their proximity into an intimate walk.

Chad grinned down at her as he unlocked the door. He was up to something, the way he impatiently rushed to get the door open. He pushed the door wide, and before Hope could step in, Chad looped his arm around her neck and one around her knee, and lifted her up off her feet. Hope laughed, wrapping her arm around his neck, pressing a sweet kiss against his cheek.

"Hey, I need to carry my bride across the threshold." Chad winked at her as he carried her inside and through to the bedroom, where he placed her on her feet.

Hope observed that the door that typically was open was closed. "What are you up to?" she asked suspiciously, as she watched his scheming eyes.

He held his hand out. "Hold on, let me sneak in there real quick. I promised I was in charge of the wedding night. Since we aren't at a romantic hotel, I had to make my own." Before Hope could object, Chad slipped into the room like a ninja. She listened to his movements in the room, but couldn't detect what he was doing.

After a few minutes, she heard the door unlock from the other side, swinging wide open. Hope watched as Chad moved to her, gently placing his hand on her upper arm to guide her inside. She pressed her hand to her mouth when she entered the room. Chad had lined the room with small candles, flickering in the dark. And the bed... the bed she was so familiar with was dressed in fresh white and cream sheets. The top was delicately designed in a heart with silk rose petals.

"Chad." Hope was speechless as she leaned into him. The room was so distinctly different than his bachelor pad she knew so well.

Chad didn't respond verbally. He pulled Hope to himself, kissing her lovingly, his arms wrapping around her intimately. He pushed her up against the wall, pressing his knee between her legs. Their kiss wasn't broken by the movement, it only grew deeper, and more intense. Chad pressed his body against hers, and when she felt like her heart was doing leaps in her chest, he broke the kiss to say the last thing they would say for the night. This was the start of an intimately passionate night, shared by a newly married couple. "I love you, Hope."

epilogue

*C*HAD PRESSED HIS HEAD AGAINST the pillow he'd positioned what seemed like a hundred times. The first night on the ship was always the hardest for him. After finding the most comfortable position in that moment, he pulled out the rectangular tan-colored envelope Hope had given him. She made him promise to open it on the first night they were on the ship. His beautiful wife knew today was going to be one of the hardest nights of the deployment.

Chad slid his index finger underneath the seal of the envelope and tore it open, and smiled as he pulled out the card. The outside picture of the card was a teddy bear. No words or greeting. Odd. He flipped it open and read the words of love she had written for him. He closed the card and opened it again, staring at her writing. He did it once more before letting the card lay on his stomach. Chad couldn't help but laugh; if he didn't laugh, he would cry. Cry with joy. He picked up the card and stared at the script once more.

Chad,
Hurry home soon. I love you.

With all my love,
Hope
P.S. You're gonna be a daddy.

Acknowledgments

FIRST AND FOREMOST, I WANT to thank **God Almighty** for blessing me abundantly in my life. The following acknowledgements and any achievement in my life is credited to you alone. Thank you.

To my **Mom**, **Dad**, **Soly,** and **Ken**, thank you for supporting every venture in my life. You have held me up and are the reason why I have such a solid concrete foundation in my life.

To **Nancee Cain**, thank you for believing in my writing before even reading a piece of it. Thank you for being a supportive author who has answered any and all of my questions. You are an incredible woman. Your writing is an inspiration of mine. I have learned so much from you alone.

To **Cat Parisi**, what can I say? Kismet crossed and we met. If it weren't for you, Fiona Tulle would not be a reality. Your constant support, your constant words of wisdom, and guidance are immeasurable. You are a special person, Cat, and I am forever grateful for you. Thank you for pulling me off that proverbial cliff over and over again. Thank you for everything you have done for me, and everything you are going to do for me. This world needs more of you, I need more of you. Your friendship has been so life changing. I love you girl, so much more than you know. I love my #TulleTribe.

To **Melissa Pascoe**, my sweet sweet sister from other parents, but I think our partnership has blossomed over a good strong cup of coffee, hehe. Thank you for being a beta first, alpha next, and now my PA. For your encouragement, and being a constant voice of reason. Thank you. You mean so much to me, that there aren't enough words to fill this book. I am so honored to call you part of my #TulleTribe. We are more alike than not, and I look forward to this adventure with you!

To **Jenn Wood**, thank you for taking on this project. Your skills for honing my story will have a lifetime effect on my story. I look forward to working with you more closely, Jenn. There really aren't words how much I appreciate you. I am honored to call you my word wizard. Thank you for always being available and answering my questions, even when you've stared at my words for hours.

To **BT Urruela**, thank you for taking the time out of your busy schedule to take these beautiful cover images. I am honored to have you on my team for Pursuing Hope. What you stand for, and represent is something I am so proud to align myself with. Your work is stunning, and I look forward to working with you again, very soon. This series is special and your work is well represented on the covers.

To **Burton & Kaitlin Hughes**, thank you so much for working with me on this project. Your chemistry shines and I couldn't ask for a better Chad and Hope than the two of you. I hope to work with you both again very soon.

To **Tiffany (TE Black Designs)**. What can I say? I am always rendered speechless with your work and talent. Thank you for caring so much about my cover design and formatting. I know you "get" my obscure visions and you bring them to life. I am your biggest fan and I can't wait to work with you on more projects.

To **Lexi C. Foss**, thank you for being my writing buddy. Thank you for your accountability and honest feedback. We may write under different tropes, but I have found a forever writing friend in you. I look forward to writing and sharing more with you!

To **Kathy R.**, **Ali C.**, **Jan D.**, thank you for being the first to hear of my story. Thank you for offering encouragement and sharing in my excitement. Your support is invaluable.

To my wonderful betas, **Kirsty Fitzpatrick**, **Barbara Shuler**, **Mary Heller, Melissa Pascoe**, and **Kelly Smith**, thank you so much for taking your time to read my first book. Your feedback has made *Pursuing Hope* a reality.

To the authors who have offered advice and wisdom along the way, it has been such a welcoming experience. Your words are gold, and I will forever support your ventures as you have mine.

To all the men and women who serve in our military. This series is written for you. I see your sacrifice, I see your life, and I value it. Thank you for those who serve, served, and will serve. You have my heart.

about *Fiona Tulle*

FIONA TULLE HAS ALWAYS HAD a love for writing, from a very young age. She uses her words as an escape from the day to day, getting lost in her characters' worlds. When not writing she can be found curled up with her pups, reading her favorite books in the sunshine of Northeast Florida.

She is an avid photography lover and loves hiding behind a camera as well. One day she dreams of having her own images gracing her covers.

LEARN MORE ABOUT FIONA TULLE:

www.facebook.com/fionatulle
www.facebook.com/groups/koffehaus
www.goodreads.com/fionatulle
www.twitter.com/fionatulle